INSULT TO INJURY

Praise for Gun Brooke

Wayworn Lovers

"*Wayworn Lovers* is a super dramatic, angsty read, very much in line with Brooke's other contemporary romances…I'm definitely in the 'love them' camp."—*The Lesbian Review*

Thorns of the Past

"What I really liked from the offset is that Brooke steered clear of the typical butch PI with femme damsel in distress trope. Both main characters are what I would call ordinary women—they both wear suits for work, they both dress down in sweatpants and sweatshirts in the evening. As a result, I instantly found it a lot easier to relate, and connect with both. Each of their pasts hold dreadful memories and pain, and the passages where they opened up to each other about those events were very moving."—*Rainbow Reviews*

"I loved the romance between Darcy and Sabrina and the story really carried it well, with each of them learning that they have a safe haven with the other."—*The Lesbian Review*

Soul Unique

"This is the first book that Gun Brooke has written in a first person perspective, and that was 100% the correct choice. She avoids the pitfalls of trying to tell a story about living with an autism spectrum disorder that she's never experienced, instead making it the story of someone who falls in love with a person living with Asperger's… *Soul Unique* is her best. It was an ambitious project that turned out beautifully. I highly recommend it."—*The Lesbian Review*

"Yet another success from Gun Brooke. The premise is interesting, the leads are likeable and the supporting characters are well-developed. The first person narrative works well, and I really enjoyed reading about a character with Asperger's."—*Melina Bickard, Librarian, Waterloo Library (London)*

The Blush Factor

"Gun Brooke captures very well the two different 'worlds' the two main characters live in and folds this setting neatly into the story. So, if you are looking for a well-edited, multi-layered romance with engaging characters this is a great read and maybe a re-read for those days when comfort food is a must."—*Lesbians on the Loose*

Fierce Overture

"Gun Brooke creates memorable characters, and Noelle and Helena are no exception. Each woman is 'more than meets the eye' as each exhibits depth, fears, and longings. And the sexual tension between them is real, hot, and raw."—*Just About Write*

September Canvas

"In this character-driven story, trust is earned and secrets are uncovered. Deanna and Faythe are fully fleshed out and prove to the reader each has much depth, talent, wit and problem-solving abilities. *September Canvas* is a good read with a thoroughly satisfying conclusion."—*Just About Write*

Lambda Literary Award Finalist *Sheridan's Fate*

"Sheridan's fire and Lark's warm embers are enough to make this book sizzle. Brooke, however, has gone beyond the wonderful emotional explorations of these characters to tell the story of those who, for various reasons, become differently-abled. Whether it is a bullet, an illness, or a problem at birth, many women and men find themselves in Sheridan's situation. Her courage and Lark's gentleness and determination send this romance into a 'must read.'"—*Just About Write*

Coffee Sonata

"In *Coffee Sonata*, the lives of these four women become intertwined. In forming friendships and love, closets and disabilities are discussed, along with differences in age and backgrounds. Love and friendship are areas filled with complexity and nuances. Brooke takes her time to savor the complexities while her main characters savor their excellent cups of coffee. If you enjoy a good love story, a great setting, and wonderful characters, look for *Coffee Sonata* at your favorite gay and lesbian bookstore."—*Family & Friends Magazine*

"Award-winning author Gun Brooke has given us another delightful romance with *Coffee Sonata*. I was so totally immersed in this story that I read it in one sitting."—*Just About Write*

"Each of these characters is intriguing, attractive and likeable, but they are heartbreaking, too, as the reader soon learns when their pasts and their deeply buried secrets are slowly and methodically revealed. Brooke does not give the reader predictable plot points, but builds a fascinating set of subplots and surprises around the romances."—*L-word.com Literature*

Course of Action

"Brooke's words capture the intensity of their growing relationship. Her prose throughout the book is breathtaking and heart-stopping. Where have you been hiding, Gun Brooke? I, for one, would like to see more romances from this author."—*Independent Gay Writer*

"The setting created by Brooke is a glimpse into that fantasy world of celebrity and high rollers, escapist to be sure, but witnessing the relationship develop between Carolyn and Annelie is well worth the trip. As the reader progresses, the trappings become secondary to the characters' desire to reach goals both professional and personal."
—*Midwest Book Review*

"The characters are the strength of *Course Of Action* and are the reason why I keep coming back to it again and again. Carolyn and Annelie are smart, strong, successful women who have come up from difficult pasts. Their chemistry builds slowly as they get to know each other, and the book satisfyingly leaves them in an established relationship, each having grown and been enriched by the other. I love every second that the two spend together."
—*The Lesbian Review*

Escape: Exodus Book Three

"I've been a keen follower of the Exodus series for a while now and I was looking forward to the latest installment. It didn't disappoint. The action was edge-of-your-seat thrilling, especially towards the end, with several threats facing the Exodus mission. Some very intriguing subplots were introduced, and I look forward to reading more about these in the next book."—*Melina Bickard, Librarian, Waterloo Library, London (UK)*

Pathfinder: Exodus Book Two

"I love Gun Brooke. She has successfully merged two of my reading loves: lesfic and sci-fi."—*Inked Rainbow Reads*

Advance: Exodus Book One

"*Advance* is an exciting space adventure, hopeful even through times of darkness. The romance and action are balanced perfectly, interesting the audience as much in the fleet's mission as in Dael and Spinner's romance. I'm looking forward to the next book in the series!"—*All Our Worlds: Diverse Fantastic Fiction*

The Supreme Constellations Series

"*Protector of the Realm* has it all; sabotage, corruption, erotic love and exhilarating space fights. Gun Brooke's second novel is forceful with a winning combination of solid characters and a brilliant plot. The book exemplifies her growth as inventive storyteller and is sure to garner multiple awards in the coming year."—*Just About Write*

Protector of the Realm "is first and foremost a romance, and whilst it has action and adventure, it is the romance that drives it.The book moves along at a cracking pace, and there is much happening throughout to make it a good page-turner. The action sequences are very well done, and make for an adrenaline rush."—*The Lesbian Review*

"Brooke is an amazing author. Never have I read a book where I started at the top of the page and don't know what will happen two paragraphs later. She keeps the excitement going, and the pages turning."—*Family and Friends Magazine*

By the Author

INSULT TO INJURY

by
Gun Brooke

2019

INSULT TO INJURY

ISBN 13: 978-1-63555-323-9

This Trade Paperback Original Is Published By
Bold Strokes Books, Inc.
P.O. Box 249
Valley Falls, NY 12185

First Edition: July 2019

CREDITS
EDITOR: SHELLEY THRASHER
PRODUCTION DESIGN: STACIA SEAMAN
COVER DESIGN BY GUN BROOKE AND SHERI (HINDSIGHTGRAPHICS@GMAIL.COM)

Acknowledgments

The main characters in this book made it so rewarding—and sometimes also so emotional—to write. Thank you especially to Elon for helping me "snap out of it" when I needed to. And also, I have to mention my dogs, Hoshi and Esti, without whose unconditional love, life wouldn't be the same and writing a book like this one would be harder.

Thank you to Shelley Thrasher, my editor, without whom I would not fare as well as a writer. After all these novels together, it is still such a treat to work with you. I am in such great hands.

I never take for granted the fact that I am among the lucky few in this world that get to write stories and be published by a dedicated, enthusiastic publisher. Thank you, Len Barot (Radclyffe), for your continued faith in me.

Sandy Lowe, senior editor, is the excellent, amazing hub of BSB—and a great person to contact when necessary. Cindy, Ruth, Carsen, and the rest of the BSBers—you're all rock stars and I truly appreciate everything you do.

My first readers/beta readers—you are my first safety net. I truly appreciate your feedback, pointers, rescue attempts, and encouragement. I cannot tell you enough how much I appreciate you taking time out of your life to read through my chapters. Thank you!

Family, friends, and readers—you all have your designated places in my heart. Thank you for encouraging words and for sharing the joy of storytelling with me.

For Elon

PROLOGUE

Romi

"Sit there and don't move." The female cop sounds gruff, and her eyes are hard when she motions toward a bench where two men are sitting handcuffed with their hands on their backs. I'm cuffed too, but at least with my hands in front of me. Trembling, I obey.

"Officer?" I plead. "Please. What am I accused of?"

"Just sit tight. And I'm watching you." The cop glares at me, and I know I'm seconds away from being cuffed like the guys. The fact that I'm not may be because I'm five foot two and scrawny. I probably look to her as if she can restrain me with one hand while she eats her lunch with the other.

I cling to the faux leather bag in my lap, as it holds all my worldly possessions. The cop has already searched it but found nothing she was interested in. She looked mildly surprised at the worn notebook where I jot down notes every day in super-tiny handwriting. That way it lasts me a long time. I keep sharpening the pencil when I write for that purpose. Pencils are cheap, and sometimes I prioritize, using the money I make singing in the subway to buy them instead of food.

"I've seen you around," one of the young men beside me says, not unkindly. "You're that singer."

I'm not sure whether to feel flattered or freaked out. Who

knows why he's here in cuffs? If the cops let him go—and me—what if he comes looking for me?

"Mmm," I say noncommittally.

"You've got a good voice. Why're you here?"

"No clue." I turn to him and see nothing but friendliness in his eyes. Blue eyes nearly void of pupils show he's on something, but he looks more dazed than someone who's about to go postal. "You?"

"Possession." He nods to his back pocket as if whatever he's on is still there, but of course it's not. The cops must've searched him. "Same ol', same ol'."

I have never fallen into the trap of doing drugs. With too many other problems, it seemed illogical to add to the mess that is my life. Living as a runaway from age sixteen creates enough hurdles.

"I'm Sam," the guy says.

"Romi." I nearly extend my hand to say hello but remember our handcuffs and merely do an awkward little wave with my fingertips.

"Come on, now." The cop is back. "Time to take you through booking."

Booking? My heart stops long enough to make me dizzy. "But, Officer, please tell me why. I have no idea how I broke the law. What did I do?" I walk obediently next to her, not wanting to do anything to make things worse, but so afraid that I'm shaking.

"All right, since you ask politely, unlike most I bring in." Tall and with her brown hair in a tight bun, she stops and looks down at me. "Your wallet containing your expired ID was found at the scene of a B&E on the Upper East Side. A lot was stolen. You were identified by a police officer working in the subway, who recognized you from the photo."

My wallet? My wallet that was stolen more than a month ago. And what the hell was a B&E? Breaking and entering? "But…my wallet was stolen. I had eight dollars and forty cents in it."

"Convenient," the cop says, shaking her head.

I realize nobody is going to believe me. I haven't done anything illegal, at least nothing like that, but I'm among the lowest of the low in this city, so who's going to take my words seriously?

The cop uncuffs one of my hands, and it looks like she means to attach the open cuff to a ring on the desk. I don't know if it's my slight frame or something else that makes her underestimate me, but she takes her eyes off me long enough for me to see my chance. A group of cops is heading our way, pushing four large young men along, and these guys aren't cooperating. My cop is knocked aside but jumps into the fray to assist her colleagues by slamming one of the men into the wall. I see my brief window of opportunity the moment the thudding sound of bodies clashing against each other and into walls, and voices yelling out commands, attract all interest in the room.

I push my worn jacket off and fold it over my arm and hand to hide the dangling cuffs. I snatch an even worse-looking baseball cap from the head of a young boy that sits cuffed on a chair in front of my cop's desk and put it on. It reeks of unwashed hair. The kid shouts something in protest, but all the noise drowns out his words.

Before I make my way out of there, the last thing I see is the cops drawing their Tasers against the men—and the thumbs-up from Sam where he grins lazily at me from the bench before mouthing, "Run!"

CHAPTER ONE

Romi

The basement looks just like I remember. Nobody has moved anything since Aunt Clara resided in the old farmhouse. She used the cellar to store preserves, old magazines, and a multitude of boxes containing things she was certain she would find a use for some day. Looking at the very same boxes now, I realize she never did. Good thing she didn't change the secret spot for the spare key to the basement door either. Anyone could have found it, as hiding it above the doorframe is hardly original.

I haven't been upstairs yet. From peeking through the windows, I could tell all the furniture is covered with sheets, which means someone has bothered to take care of the place. I'm not sure when Aunt Clara died. I only found out about it when browsing the local East Quay newspaper online at the library a year ago. That suggests the house has been empty for approximately that long, unless she was hospitalized for a long time. The obituary didn't specify.

Six years ago, I ran away from my aunt's indifference and went looking for a place to belong. I never did find what I was searching for, and it's ironic that I'm back where I used to thoroughly hate my life.

I debate whether to risk going upstairs to explore but

can't come up with a reason. If the house has been uninhabited since Aunt Clara died, I won't find any food upstairs. Whoever maintains the house must have cleared out the upstairs pantry and fridge. Down here, though, I see row after row of preserves. I look at the large chest freezer in the far corner. Could I be so lucky? I walk over, and just as I start to open it, I stop in mid-motion. The general power is off and probably has been since my aunt passed away. Whatever is in this freezer, if anything, is long expired. If I open it, I'll just create a worse stink than the dust and dried-up sewage pipes put together.

I leave the old freezer alone and move over to the wooden shelves holding the preserves. Jam, applesauce, fruit, pickles, berries—all neatly stacked. I read the labels with some difficulty, as Aunt Clara's old-fashioned handwriting apparently became trembly and barely decipherable during her last year. Still, she kept making the most of the fruits and vegetables in the garden. The dates indicate that her last batch won't kill me. I know how careful she was, how meticulous about hygiene.

I pull out two jars of applesauce and one of pickles. I have some bread that I bought at a local baker in Westport, the village before East Quay. I walked to Aunt Clara's farmhouse from there, not wanting to stumble across anyone in East Quay who might recognize me from my high school years. Granted, I only stayed long enough to finish the fall semester of my sophomore year, but I must remember to be careful. I do look very different nowadays compared to when I was clothed by my aunt and my hair styled in a long ponytail. My short, shaggy hair and lack of style when it comes to clothes might be enough of a disguise.

Now I place the jars on a small wooden table next to a wall of metal shelving. Here, Aunt Clara's treasures are packed in neat boxes and labeled accordingly. I sometimes had to do that part, and Aunt Clara would huff and shake her head if I misspelled something or didn't apply myself when it came to proper penmanship.

I grab one of the shelves' consoles and tug gently. Nothing

happens. I stand back and examine the floor. I do have the right shelf, and the faint scratch marks on the concrete floor prove it. I tug harder on the shelf, but still nothing. A memory, very faint, pokes at me, and I stand back, trying to figure out why the shelf won't budge. I gaze up, squinting at the top shelf. Then I remember how, when I was little, I used to have to climb to reach the lever on it. Not that much taller now, I step on the first shelf and feel among the thick layer of dust for the narrow metal rod. I find it, but it's damn near impossible to move. Will I have to find something to grease it with?

Just then it shifts and swings sideways, in over the top shelf. I jump down and pull at the shelf section again. This time it swings toward me as if I'd opened it yesterday. I grab my jars and step through the narrow opening. I let the shelf remain open, as I don't know if the lever on this side will work just as well.

The narrow room is fully equipped, just like Aunt Clara's husband planned it in the sixties. The floor is set deeper into the ground, so I have to go down four steps before I reach it. In here it's not made of concrete, but hardwood. I spot the familiar twin bed to the right. A sealed plastic bag holds bedding and blankets, and a thick plastic sheet covers the foam mattress. Aunt Clara showed me early on how to take the mattress out once every three months and air it after smacking it with a rug beater. I was always afraid of that thing because Aunt Clara had made clear once and for all, when I came to live with her at age four, that she could use it for doing much more than beating rugs. I understood quite well that I had to be a very good girl in this house, or Aunt Clara might use the rug beater on me.

On the right side of the room, a small door leads into a fully functional shower and toilet. I open the door and peer inside. It's dark and smells horrible, but not like a dead rodent or anything that foul. I flush the toilet, and at first, I think it's broken, as no water runs into the bowl. But then the top part starts to fill, and the next time I press the handle, discolored water enters the bowl and levels out. I pee, glad to see four rolls of toilet paper on the shelf next to where I sit. I flush again, and this time the discoloration is less pronounced, or so I guess, since the light coming down the stairs from the basement lets me see very little.

The room has no windows, of course, only air vents with huge filters, which Aunt Clara showed me how to clean in the shower. Remembering the shower, I let the water run there, and it's all cold, of course. The furnace isn't operational, but the idea of having my own shower, even a cold one, makes me smile. I can get water because of the solar panels Aunt Clara had installed. She was very pleased about how well they worked, not only to supply her beloved husband's nuclear-bomb shelter with electricity, but the entire house.

I flip the switch for the light, feeling silly for not remembering about the solar panels before. A ceiling light flickers and then lights up the secret room. I go over to the bed and click on the table lamp on the nightstand. Then I turn toward the kitchen area, albeit calling it a kitchen is taking it too far. It's a kitchenette cabinet that holds a small freezer/fridge combo, a cooktop, a microwave, and storage for plates, utensils, cups, and glassware. The cabinet doors are well sealed, and it's still clean inside.

Everything in the secret room must have been untouched for quite some time, unless Aunt Clara had the energy to keep it up until she died, and still it looks as pristine as when I saw it last. The only thing new to me is the microwave. I check under the bed. Oh, yes. There's the generator that can be run using petrol or, if need be, hooked up to an exercise bike that sits at the foot of the bed. Its exhaust tube is connected to the ventilation shaft. That was her husband Julian's original idea, and of course Aunt Clara maintained it religiously.

I open the fridge hesitantly, afraid to find some stinky mess in there, but it's empty and clean. Of course. I place the jars inside and switch it on. Once I open them, they will need to stay refrigerated.

Making the bed is both therapeutic and practical. I'm surprised at the scent of lavender emanating from the plastic bag containing the sheets and blankets, until I remember how fanatic Aunt Clara was when it came to placing the dried plants in drawers and cabinets. I can't remember when I last felt such nice bedding against my skin. Probably six years ago, in this house. The places I've slept since then have offered everything from coarse fabrics in shelters, to cardboard boxes under overpasses. No, that's not true. There was that time when someone tried to mug an old lady in the subway, in the car where I was singing, and the guy knocked me over when he tried to escape. I hit the back of my head on an armrest that had been robbed of its padding and spent two nights in the hospital after they stitched me up. Those sheets were nice, but nowhere near as soft as these.

I realize I've put it off long enough. I must get my act together and walk upstairs. If nothing else, I could visit my old room, if it's still intact, and carry down some of my stuff. Nervous as hell now, I remind myself to breathe before I climb the few steps to the basement and then face the stairs leading up to the main floor. It's a large house.

The ground floor consists of a large hallway, a spacious country kitchen, two rooms for entertainment, and my late uncle's study, which Aunt Clara referred to as the library after he passed away. I was never allowed in there unaccompanied since my aunt was sure I would mess things up—and God forbid I would want to take a book to my room to read. I honestly didn't care since I was the local library's best customer back then. Perhaps I can get a new library card… I realize what I'm doing and backpedal that thought. I have no ID. Not even my expired one. No chance in hell I can get a library card.

Sad and frustrated, I slowly make my way up the stairs to the ground floor. Curtains I don't recognize are drawn close inside the windows, giving the rooms an eerie, misty ambiance. Getting closer, I see bed sheets flipped over the curtain rods. Behind them, my aunt's drapes are still there, ever flowery and very pink. This meant she left this house, either when going into hospital or after dying at home, during the spring or summer. Had it been during the fall or winter, the drapes left behind would have been navy, green, or maroon velvet.

Walking through the hallway, I feel like I'm moving through a ghost house. The sheets covering furniture and windows make everything look alien and eerie. Dust floats in the air, probably because I'm the first in a long time to stir it up.

I take the stairs up to the next floor, steeling myself against what I may find when I open the door to the room that used to be mine. Holding my breath, I walk toward it, my steps slowing as I see it's already wide open. Of course it is. Why wouldn't it be? I used to keep it closed all the time, whether I was in there or not.

I stop on the threshold and peer into the room where I lived from age four until I turned sixteen. Everything is covered in sheets, but it's also so familiar. Each outline under the dusty covers shows me that my furniture, and perhaps also my belongings, are there. An unexpected sound makes me jump, but then I realize it's my own breathing. Why has Aunt Clara kept this up? Did she hope I'd return? The idea makes my throat ache, as if many years' worth of tears have gathered there to choke me.

I cross the room to the shelf at the far end. Carefully trying not to disturb the dust, I lift the sheet that covers my old bookshelf. When I see my old books, bought with my own money that I earned from babysitting, lawn mowing, and such, I whimper again. This time the sound leaving my throat is half joyful and half full of...remorse?

I run my right index finger along the spines while I push the sheet out farther with my left hand. Picking out five titles I'm dying to reread, I tuck them into my jacket pocket, as I'm still wearing the thrift-shop bargain I scored two months ago. Two dollars gave me a gray jacket with a faux fur-lined hood and, best of all, with two huge pockets and four small ones.

I poke my head into each of the other three bedrooms, and they too look the same as before, though covered up.

Back on the ground floor, I hesitate again. I might never have been allowed in my uncle's study, but I've seen it from the doorway enough times to know about the walls and walls of books. What kind did he and my aunt read? I'm curious enough to approach the double doors, which, unlike the others in the house, are closed. This gives me pause, but then I decide it's pure coincidence. The sliding doors, old and made of massive oak, are a bit difficult to move but eventually slide open. I take one step inside the study—and just stare.

On the impressive desk, also made of oak, sits a computer screen. My aunt was against all such things, never even had a cell phone or, God forbid, a TV. Yet here's what looks like a state-of-the-art machine with a screen that must be at least twenty-six inches wide and a midi tower. The keyboard and the mouse are both cordless.

When I raise my eyes and look around me, goose bumps erupt on my arms. No sheets anywhere. The bookshelves, holding almost more books than they can take, are free of dust. Looking down at the floors I can see they're clean as well, except where my now-dusty soles have left prints. Afraid now, I crouch and wipe the dust off as I back out of the room. Now I notice the rest of the hardwood floors. They too have footprints, but not just mine. Other shoes have created patterns all over them. How recent are they, and why are they here? And is the computer theirs?

I make sure to close the doors after examining the dust-free floor in the study. Hurrying down the stairs and uncertain why I'm in a hurry, I try to think logically. Perhaps the house was let out to someone? Or sold? The fact that only one room has been cleaned and outfitted mystifies me.

When I'm back in the basement I draw a deep sigh of relief. I put the books on the table in the bunker and head up to fetch a few more jars of fruit and pickles. I arrange the remaining jars so it's not obvious that someone's been stealing food.

Testing the lever from inside the movable shelf, I decide I can rely on it to open when I need to leave the room. If it fails permanently, this space will become my tomb. Nobody would ever find me down here, at least not until it was too late. This is still my best option. If the cops get ahold of me, they'll charge me with breaking and entering, and, I'm pretty sure, for my successful escape.

I close the hidden shelf door from the inside of the bunker. After looking at it for five seconds and praying it won't get stuck, I open it again. It works much better now than it did the first time I tried from the other side.

Relieved, I start to laugh and return to my jars, still giggling. I open one containing pickles, pulling one out with a fork I find in a drawer. Digging my teeth into it, in a second, I'm transported back to life with my aunt. The pickle tastes great and I wolf it down relentlessly. The second pickle is more for savoring the taste. It takes me back, for the umpteenth time today, and I can hear Aunt Clara's voice, watch her eyes harden whenever she laid eyes on me, and feel reduced to nobody in particular in an instant.

I don't let those memories stop me. The pickle still tastes great.

Chapter Two

Gail

If my hand didn't hurt so bad, I'd slam it against the steering wheel. I check the damn GPS, but it doesn't make sense. The female voice my former assistant programmed for me, some famous actress with a tone that grates on my nerves, has sounded increasingly annoyed with me the last half hour. I know that's all in my head, but, honestly, the way she says, "In three hundred yards, take a *right*" has a silent "for the love of God" at the end.

I've been to the house twice but never driven there myself. My sense of direction is not the best, never has been, and I rely solely on the well-modulated, stuck-up voice coming from my GPS. Now she tells me to do a legal U-turn—and I clench my jaws. Of course, it's a legal U-turn—we're out in the sticks, for God's sake.

I know I'm on the right track when I see the two oaks flanking an unassuming, old farmhouse. Light gray, with meticulously well-kept shingles, a black roof, and fruit trees and berry bushes surrounding it, it sits on a slight hill overlooking the fields around it. A neighboring farmer leases the fields for grazing or crops. The previous owner, a widow without children, had made that arrangement more than twenty years ago, according to the will. As she had no heirs, the woman, Mrs. Delaney, left it all to the local cancer association, which in turn listed it with all its inventory.

I turn into the gravel driveway and park the car close to the front door. I have a few suitcases, and as I can use only my good left hand, I need to be near the entryway. I glare at the orthosis around my right hand. The hand that used to run the bow across the strings of my Draskóczy violin is now utterly useless. One car crash, four surgeries, and here I am, withdrawing from the world I knew and loved…for this.

I step out of the car and just stand still for a moment. The air is fresh, almost crisp. Not even Central Park in Manhattan smells like this. I inhale and place this quality on the plus side of my mental pros and cons list. Deciding to explore before I carry anything inside, I fish out the keys from the pocket of my crepe-wool Burberry coat. After I climb the two steps onto the porch, I push open the screen door and unlock the wooden one. Inside I can smell the dust, as if it's hanging in midair. I clear my throat and stride toward the double sliding door where I know my former assistant has had a tech professional install a computer and someone else in to clean the room. I certainly didn't intend to dust off all those books. The study is as I remember. Masculine, a bit old-fashioned, but cozy with the open fireplace in the inner corner.

I take off the coat and fold it over a worn leather armchair that faces the fireplace. I hope the electricity has been turned on as planned. Pressing the button on the computer tower, I see it start to boot, and within fifteen seconds I'm not just up and running, but also online. Good. Cable and internet access will make life a little easier, hopefully.

Curious about what I may not have noticed during my previous two visits, I walk through the rooms on the ground floor. I want to tear down the sheets that cover everything, but not while dressed in my trouser suit. And I have a cleaning crew coming tomorrow, which means I only have to get the master bedroom decent enough to sleep in. According to the Realtor, there's a fully stocked cleaning cabinet somewhere. I hope for a good vacuum cleaner.

Upstairs, I locate the master bedroom and realize it's bigger than I remember, with a new memory-foam, king-size bed; a large, Narnia-looking wardrobe; and a rustic vanity with a large oval mirror. Neither of the latter fits my taste, but I must admit that they fit in this room. The Realtor agreed to switch all the mattresses in the house, which proved to me that selling this countryside gem wasn't entirely easy.

I walk into the bathroom and turn on the faucets and flush the toilet twice. The smell isn't as bad as when I was here last, so perhaps the Realtor or the seller has showed up to deal with the plumbing.

Farthest down the hallways I find a small bedroom that has entirely skipped my mind. I enter and curiously lift the sheets covering the furniture, then stare as I come across what looks like a young girl's desk. I see schoolbooks, pens, writing pads, small knickknacks, and stickers. I forget about my fancy suit and tug at the sheet covering a narrow bookshelf. I think I recognize it as a Billy shelf from Ikea. It's filled with all kinds of books, most of them cheap paperbacks, but also other books the former inhabitant of this room must have bought used, judging from how old they are. The genres vary from young adult to romances and thrillers. I find some science fiction and fantasy as well, but most of the books seem to be coming-of-age stories.

Who lived here with the old woman? Where is she? I'm quite sure it's a girl's room, but of course, I shouldn't be prejudiced about pink and purple, the stickers, and the knickknacks. I'm sure boys can appreciate them too. For now, I'm going to refer to this enigmatic room as the girl's room. Apprehensively, I open a drawer in the desk and find a small stack of notebooks. Not about to pry further, I push it closed. Whoever wrote in those books and adorned the unremarkable white desk with stickers of horses, music notes, and famous people shouldn't have their privacy invaded, even though I am the legal owner of all the inventory.

The other rooms are as I remember, and I make my way down the stairs. I'm glad I parked so close. Now I can haul my bags in and change into much more appropriate attire. I have two bags of groceries to hold me over the first week. I carry my bags in, one at a time, and when I return for the cooler that holds my frozen goods, I stop as I reach the car. Someone's watching the house, or me, from the road leading to the driveway. I squint as the late fall sun is half in my eyes. It looks like a young man, no, a young woman. I attempt to ignore her and try to hoist the cooler out of the back seat.

Clearly, I've forgotten how heavy it is, and I drop the damn thing half an inch from my toes. Muttering under my breath, I see I've forgotten the cable that attaches the cooler to an outlet in my car. I unplug it and manage to hit the orthosis against the door opening when I back out.

"Hi there. Can I help you with that?" The female, hesitant voice makes me jerk back. I can see this woman is quite young and dressed in clean, but unmatched, worn clothes.

"Who are you?" I ask in my no-nonsense, terse tone.

"Um. I'm Romi. I saw you struggle with the luggage and thought I might be able to help you." She smiles hesitantly, showing off even teeth.

"Why?" I place my good hand on my hip, a pose that puts the fear of God into even the most demonic conductors. I've worked with all the greats and refuse to let any of them intimidate me.

"Just trying to be a good, you know, neighbor?" Romi shifts where she stands, but she's not even close to being intimidated, merely helpful and direct. On any other day, I might have admired that trait, but today it merely annoys me.

"You live near here?" I look around even though I've been told the closest house isn't within sight.

"Yes." Romi averts her eyes and looks down at the offending cooler. "Wow. That's a mother of a cooler you've got there...um, I didn't catch your name?"

God. I really don't want to be forced to constantly turn away odd people wanting to welcome me to the area and *socialize*. "Gail." No surname needed as she didn't give hers.

"I don't mind helping. It's not like I'm asking you to pay me," Romi says. "Just being neighborly."

I study the girl for a few moments. Her alto voice with a New England accent also holds some New York City tone. How old is she? Twenty? That's what her physical appearance suggests, but her eyes indicate an older soul. "Very well. Thank you. I appreciate it." I know I still sound like a barely harnessed bitch, but that's as gentle as I get these days.

"No problem. You're injured." Romi nods at my hand and then hoists the cooler after wrapping the cord up first. She carries it across the porch and then stops at the half-open door. "Kitchen, I assume?"

"Yes. To the left."

"Oh." Romi flinches but then nods and disappears into the house. I take the last bag out of the car and make a face at the contents. My pain medication and ointments for the fucking hand. I hate being dependent on those things. What's more, I hate my hand. It's not recognizable as mine anymore.

"There. I put it on two kitchen chairs for you. Easier to empty it that way." Romi comes to a stop after she's descended the few steps.

"Thank you." I try to sound, if not friendly, at least polite. It was considerate of her to go the extra mile like that.

"No problem," Romi says again and kicks the dirt. "I'll be on my way. Welcome to the neighborhood, such as it is."

"Well." I merely nod. Her words make me wonder for a few moments what she could possibly mean, but then I push the question away. As I walk through my front door, I turn to close it, reluctantly curious to see which way Romi's house is located. I blink, frowning. The view from the front of my house is at least a hundred yards in three directions, and Romi is already out of sight.

CHAPTER THREE

Romi

I enter the house in the way that I've practiced for the last week. Quick through the shrubbery obscuring the view from the house, to the basement door, being sure I don't make any obvious footprints anywhere and locking the door from inside, but not with the deadbolt, of course. Gail has the regular basement key, and if suddenly the deadbolt is used, and she's not the one doing it, that would be disastrous. Luckily, I have keys for both.

Gail. It's been a week now, and I've concluded that I've never met anyone like her. She's older than me, that's obvious, but I have no idea by how much. I'd say she's in her mid or late thirties, but I'm not good at guessing ages. She has blond hair that reaches her shoulders in a soft curve. It looks thick and has that shine to it you get from using fancy shampoos and conditioners. I once scored some sample bottles of that stuff and loved the way my black hair suddenly had bluish highlights and how it curved easily against my head. I keep it short, mainly because it's easier to maintain, as I often don't know when and where my next shower will happen. Perhaps now since I have the shower in the bunker room, I can let it grow longer. I can shower or flush the toilet only when Gail is outside or if she's running water at the same time. Otherwise, the sound of the pipes will give me away.

I admit that trying to learn more about my involuntary landlady, which is a ridiculous word for someone as posh and haughty as Gail, is starting to take up more of my time. That, and the undeniable guilt of trespassing. If I could do this differently, I would, but I can't think of any other way. The cops will never take my word for not being part of the breaking and entering. I've been to the library in Westport, twice, using the computers. I pick the time when the high school kids swarm the place. They're not always so interested in the computers as they're always on their cell phones anyway. It also makes it easier for me to blend in and not risk anyone suddenly asking for a library card.

When I looked at the crime reports from New York City, mainly from the online newspapers, I found two snippets that I thought could be about me. The breaking and entering I read about took place in a wealthy area, and the thieves stole super-expensive watches and jewelry, among other things, from some bigwig. No way a New York newspaper would report a robbery if it was just about a regular person. This had to be someone important, which means I'm even more screwed because they're not going to let the theft grow cold. No way. The second snippet told that a person of interest in the high-profile robbery had escaped police custody during a "spectacular maneuver." Ha. Spectacular, my ass. I walked out of there because the cops dropped the ball and took their eyes off me. I'm not going to prison because some idiot planted my wallet at the scene of a crime. I'm just grateful that nobody who lived in that house got hurt. At least I couldn't find any reports of that. And I doubt that cop would have handled me quite that unassumingly if that were the case.

I listen as I'm in the basement, to make sure Gail hasn't stepped back into the house. I saw her briefly through the branches where she was walking slowly at the far end of the yard, wrapped in a blanket and holding a steaming mug with her good hand. I wonder what happened to her. If I wanted to, I could probably research who bought the house and find out things about her, but that would make me feel like more of a creep than I already do.

I try to console myself with the fact that I don't sneak around in hollow walls and eavesdrop on the poor woman. I keep tabs on her only when she showers so I can get clean too. That is perhaps a tiny bit creepy, but I've got to be careful.

I begin to pull at the shelf when I hear steps above me. I stop and hold my breath. Gail sure came back inside quickly. I was waiting in the shrubbery for a while until she exited the house via the deck on the back. She could have been out there with the mug for only three or four minutes.

I hear murmurs and then her voice almost as clear as if she were standing right next to me. Before I freak out, I look up and see a grid by the ceiling. Right. That's the spy vent. I'd forgotten about that. Whenever Aunt Clara was on the phone with someone at school about something I'd done, or not done, she would sit in her armchair by the far corner of the living room. She called it her parlor, which sounded ridiculous to me. When she was in that corner, I would sit right here and overhear her part of the conversation.

I know I should remove myself and not inadvertently spy on Gail, but I'm afraid to move. It's only logical to assume the sound travels both ways. Groaning inwardly, I try sticking my fingers in my ear, but as I can't go "la-la-la-la-la" to drown out the words filtering through from above, I can still hear Gail speak. And, boy, does she sound pissed.

"I have told them too many times, Neill. No, I'm not interested in any further tests. I swear, each time they've had their incompetent hands all over my arm, not to mention the torture they call physiotherapy, I've only gotten worse." Gail spits the words and her frustration is palpable. "No. I—said—no."

I wonder who this Neill is, who is brave, or foolish, enough to contradict this woman. A family member? Perhaps. Gail is quiet, and I'm not sure if she hung up on the dude or if she's listening. Turns out to be the latter.

"How dare you?" Now Gail's frustration has morphed into fury. "How dare you even ask me that? I might expect that from pretty much anyone else, but not you. Of course I bloody miss it!" A thump on the floor suggests Gail may have stomped her foot. I wouldn't have pegged her as a stomper, but I suppose enough anger might need that type of outlet. "I miss playing every single day. If you think the pain of not even being able to look at my violin will make me subject myself to the agony of yet another surgery, and yet another clueless surgeon out to make a name for himself by becoming my savior, you're not the friend I thought you were. I have to go."

Everything becomes quiet after that. I still don't dare to move. She spoke the last sentences with so much anguish in her voice that my heart raced. I'm not sure why her anger and pain affect me. I mean, I don't know her at all, but they do.

I hear her footsteps as she walks to the other end of the house. Relieved, I grab hold of the shelf again and pull at it slowly. I manage to move it only an inch when I hear her steps as she walks down the stairs to the basement.

Panic-stricken, I gaze around me, unable to think. Getting the shelf open enough to slip through isn't an option. Too slow and too loud. My head swivels enough to make the muscles in my neck spasm as I look for an escape. I spot Aunt Clara's large oak chest, which apparently her ancestors brought to America from Europe. It used to be empty. I tiptoe over to it and open the lid. It squeaks, but I have to chance it. I jump into the chest and find that it holds some fabrics, but I believe I can curl up enough to fit. Not the first time I'm glad I'm not a large person.

I pull the lid down over me, where I'm in a fetal position on my side. The lid won't close enough, which leaves a half-inch gap. I can see the basement with my left eye and pray Gail won't notice it.

"Damn," Gail mutters to herself and runs her good hand through her hair. She keeps it loose today. Some other days she's worn it in an austere twist. I wonder how she manages that with just one hand. "Was the old lady a hoarder?"

Not far from it, but not like the people on the TV shows I've caught on library computers and the TVs at the shelters. Aunt Clara kept things, and since she'd done so for a very long time, of course the place got cluttered. She did make sure everything was neat and tidy, which was another one of her mantras, which I know from personal experience. I dusted and cleaned this basement and everything in it more than once when I lived here.

I breathe as quietly as I can while I watch Gail move around down here. She raises a lid here and there, and I just know my luck's about to run out. Even if I could prove my innocence when it came to that robbery, which I doubt, I couldn't swear myself free of this invasion. I haven't broken anything, but I have entered—and I have stolen food. In the eyes of cops, that would be strike two.

I nearly gasp when Gail reads the labels on the jars of fruit and pickles. She tilts her head, and her hair falls to the side like a golden curtain. "Plums, cherries, applesauce...not bad." She takes a jar from the shelf and casts another glance around the room. I can swear she looks right into my eye when she spots the chest.

I'm shaking now, and if she comes closer, I'm sure she'll hear my shoes reverberate against the massive wood. I really hope she won't. I don't want to scare her. Finding a person in a chest in your own basement could give anyone nightmares for years. I squeeze my eyes shut as if that will help ward Gail off somehow. Kind of like those three monkeys. See no evil...

When nothing happens, I open my eyes slowly after a few moments, and I'm alone in the basement. As I'm in the chest, I can't hear if she's walking up the stairs, but after waiting another couple of minutes, I deduce that she must have. I push the lid up very slowly, afraid I'll drop it and it'll slam into the wall behind it. My legs ache from being folded up so tight, and I nearly fall when I climb out of the chest. It feels like escaping a damn coffin. I walk quietly toward my bookshelf, and looking at it, I'm grateful that she didn't notice how misaligned it was. It sticks out more than an inch, and if Gail had examined it, she would have seen how it ends in a thirty-degree angle to be able to swing free of the neighboring shelf.

I open it, only as much as I must to slip through, and pull it closed behind me. Only when I'm inside do I realize I forgot to listen if Gail was back in the spy corner. If she was, and heard me moving the shelf, she might be down to investigate. At least she won't find me lurking here, though—I stop my train of thought. Did I close the lid to the chest?

I hate when I start second-guessing myself. I'm not going to risk opening the shelf when I don't know where Gail is in the house. If she comes down and sees the lid to the chest open, I'm sure she would freak out a bit, but surely when she found nothing wrong, *she* would be the one second-guessing herself. I know I'm grasping at straws, but I'm desperate for some shelter where I can regroup and find some sort of solution to the trouble I'm in. Then I'll be out of Gail's beautiful hair, and she'll never even know I was ever in it.

Gail

I'm still seething after hanging up on Neill. As my friend, he should know better than to underestimate me, and as my agent, he should know better than to try to maneuver me. Yes, Neill, unlike other people in my life, has always been the one I can tolerate more from, when it comes to personal matters. His sarcastic sense of humor is almost always witty, and I appreciate having someone whom I don't scare the living daylights out of. I suppose I shouldn't be surprised that most of my peers, and definitely all the younger musicians I've worked with, walk on eggshells around me. I don't suffer fools with any sort of patience, and my striving for perfection over the years has given me the reputation of being a four-star bitch.

I'm not impulsive and I don't get angry. That's not it. I know I can be scathing and even more sarcastic than Neill, and I expect everyone to do their best—and their best to be perfect. But I demand even more of myself.

Well. *Demanded.* Nowadays, my demands of perfection have sunk to an entirely different level. If I can manage a shower, blow-dry my hair, and get dressed without having to take an extra Vicodin, then I'm on the right track. It's bittersweet, no, just bitter, really, having had to lower my standards.

I toss the cell phone onto the small table in the hallway and walk into the kitchen. A crew of five has meticulously cleaned the house. They went over everything except the basement. They were supposed to clear out that space, but when they had finished working in the rest of the house, I was sick and tired of stumbling over a polishing, vacuuming, window-washing person in every room for two days, so I told them the basement could wait.

Opening a cabinet, I take out a mug, which, like everything else, came with the house. It's a ghastly orange color with purple flowers, but it holds my coffee, which is all I care about. I hold on to the mug with my good hand, sipping from it carefully as I stroll through the rooms.

I'm so bored, so frustrated, and I'm doubting my decision to flee to the countryside more and more. Sitting down in the chair where I blew up at Neill, I place the mug on the dainty side table next to it. Holding my injured, battered hand against me, I tip my head back. I rarely cry, and certainly never in anyone else's presence, but now tears stream down my face. I sob quietly and pull my legs up. Shifting sideways, I press the left side of my face against the backrest of the chair. What am I going to do with myself?

CHAPTER FOUR

Romi

I hear Gail approach the spy corner. She sits down, and after a few moments of silence, I can tell she's crying. My stomach clenches, and I have no idea why her sadness bothers me so much. Perhaps she's sad that she yelled at the person on the phone earlier. What was his name? Yes, Neill. Or she's upset that her hand is injured and she can't play...what was it? Her violin, I think.

Now she sobs, and I pull my legs up tight as I sit on the bed, sharing this stranger's agony. It rips at my soul, and I can't explain my fierce urge to protect her. What has happened to this woman, to Gail, to upset her this much? My life hasn't been stellar, but her tears speak of some fucking cataclysmic event that stole everything from her. Yes, I know that sounds dramatic, but those words fill me as I inadvertently listen to her pain.

When she finally gets up and moves to another part of the house, I sigh in relief. I haven't been close to anyone since I was four, and though I've overheard enough anxiety, grief, and sorrow in the shelters and under overpasses, nobody else's tears have impacted me like this before.

Shaking myself like dogs do, literally, as it loosens me up, I check the time on the wall clock that shows the East Coast time, Pacific time, and Greenwich Mean Time, for some reason. It's hooked up to the solar-panel wiring and works perfectly still. Six p.m. It's getting dark outside, and I need to sneak out and head to Westport. I saw a note about an open mic evening at a restaurant. It might earn me some cash and save me from having to live on fruit preserves alone.

I dress in the only decent clothes I own—black jeans with tears that look intentional, a black T-shirt with a sequined butterfly on the front. My sneakers and my army surplus jacket will have to do. I have nothing else. I regard my reflection in the bathroom mirror. My hair is okay—a little unruly in a way that can also seem like I meant for it to look like that. I have a very short stump of a kohl pen—it's one of my five sample-size pieces of makeup—and I use it sparingly around my eyes. I use everything sparingly. It's simply my way of living.

After listening carefully for a few minutes, I slowly push the shelf open toward the basement. It makes a bit of a noise, but not too bad. Closing it again, I make sure it's aligned with the rest of the shelf before I walk to the door leading out toward the garden. Not a soul in sight. Perhaps Gail has gone to lie down after being sad. I'm not sure how I figure this, but she doesn't strike me as a person who allows herself some tears very often. Life would be quite exhausting for her if that's the case.

I hurry into the bushes and disappear behind the shrubbery. If Gail has this part of the garden trimmed, I'll be in trouble. That or I'll have to do an army-crawl on my belly to the house. Yay.

The walk into Westport is rather pretty, during the daytime. Now the sun has just set, and dusk is coming. I can see fine where I walk; it's not that. It's more the long shadows cast by the trees and bushes along the way, created by the very last, faint sun rays, that spook me. I was often afraid of the dark as a kid but never dared to mention it to Aunt Clara. Sure, I tried a few times when I little, but the scornful huff at how bad such imaginings were didn't exactly encourage me to confide in her about it. It's odd that I'm feeling so secure in the basement even if there's no natural light, and if the solar panels go bye-bye, I'll be staying in a tomb. Perhaps I should try to stock up on some of those cheap batteries for LED flashlights you can get at the dollar store with the money I might make at the open mic. The owners of the restaurant won't pay anything, but some patrons might give tips if they like what they hear.

I'm relieved when I see the faint lights of the first houses on the outskirts of Westport. Energized, I lengthen my stride, and soon I feel the sidewalk under my feet, rather than the asphalt road where cars pass pedestrians way too close. They really should extend their bicycle paths around here.

It isn't hard to locate the restaurant, as quite the crowd is heading that way. Damn it. I hope they haven't filled all the slots. I may have made a huge mistake thinking that a small town like Westport wouldn't have too many hopefuls when it came to these kinds of events. I'm standing in line to enter when I realize that another line is forming more slowly next to me.

"What are you doing? Standup comedy again?" a young man asks the boy next to him, grinning.

"I have some new jokes that Dad says need a bigger audience," the boy, perhaps twelve, says, sounding precautious and, of course, adorable.

"I'm rapping one of the songs from *Hamilton*," the young man who started the conversation says.

"Cool!" High-fiving the older boy, the standup comedian whoops.

The penny drops for me. "Excuse me," I say, turning to the boys. "Is that line for the performers?"

"Sure is," the youngest says. "You entering?"

"I am." I take a step closer and place myself behind them just as two teenaged girls run up. They don't seem to mind but smile and nod.

"Like your hair," the tallest of them says.

"Thank you," I say, dumbfounded. "Your outfits are cool too." They're both dressed in long blue cloaks over black jeans and T-shirts.

"It's our choir outfit." The shorter girl twirls. "Fancy, huh?" She giggles.

"I think so." I smile faintly. It's apparently not hard to be charmed by the kids in this town.

"Haven't seen you around," the taller says, tilting her head. "Then again, I live just outside East Quay. I'm Stephanie, by the way. Stephanie Edwards-Bonnaire."

Also fancy. "I'm Romi."

"Singing?" the other girl asks. "My name's Lisa."

"Yes." I'm starting to get nervous with all this friendliness. In my experience, people are never this up front and happy-go-lucky unless they're trying to put one over on you. Still, I can't be deliberately impolite. If nothing else, that would attract too much attention to me as a person. "Nice to meet both of you."

"My moms are coming tonight to listen to us. Usually it's just Tierney, but as Giselle's, that's my other mom, well, her dog is back from the vet, so she can come for once. I hope they reserved the table over by the emergency exit for her." Frowning, Stephanie, whose explanation fails to make much sense to me, looks concerned.

Lisa nudges Stephanie. "Hey, you checked twice already."

"Yeah, you're right." Stephanie must notice that I look confused. "Giselle has agoraphobia and needs her service dog to manage. She's come so far this last year." Pride in her mother's achievement makes her beam. So, she has two moms. Awesome. I tell myself I'm not envious, but of course I would give my right hand for just one, which is ridiculous, as I'm an adult and need to focus on supporting myself—and staying out of prison.

"That's amazing," I murmur as the line begins to move. This prevents deeper conversation, and soon we're in one of the back rooms in the office area next to the kitchen, where the choir turns out to consist of ten girls between ages twelve and eighteen, from what I can see. The two boys I spoke to earlier are there, and a few other people, mainly adults. A waitress takes down our names and what we'll be performing.

"Stephanie!" A woman moves lithely between the people in the room, her long, auburn hair moving around her like falling autumn leaves.

"Hi, Tierney," Stephanie says, and then her smile dies on her lips. "What's up? Is it Giselle?"

"What? No. No!" Tierney stops next to her much-taller daughter. She gazes at each one of the choir members. "However, there's a small hiccup. Carrie can't make it. Can you sing without a leader?"

"Not again," some of the members moan. "She's barely around anymore."

"I'm sorry." Tierney wraps her arm around Stephanie's waist and another one around Lisa. "I'll talk to Manon about it. The Belmont Foundation needs to figure this out."

"We can manage for tonight," Stephanie says and juts her chin out. "Half the choir couldn't make it anyway, so we'll wing it. We're singing your song 'Fade Away.'"

Tierney beams. "Aw, you guys." She kisses Stephanie's cheek, and the pride she exudes makes my heart ache. Never, not once, have I had someone look at me with such guileless affection. And, did Stephanie say that it was Tierney's song? Like, she wrote it? Or is it merely her favorite song?

"I'm going back to the table now. Break a leg." Tierney waves to the other members as she leaves.

I walk over to a corner and try to calm my nerves. In the subway, I'm never nervous, but at open-mic nights, I can get stage fright. Not sure if it's because it's a more professional setting and that a lot of people are there to be entertained on a whole different level. In the subway, people can choose to tune you out and ignore you—but this is…yeah, different.

The choir is up just before me, according to the list one of the waitresses keeps of us. The young comedian is the last one to perform. I don't listen to the other performers at these events, normally, but this time, I'm curious about the choir. When they line up on the small stage, they look so happy, I clench my hands.

Memories of trying out for the glee club as a junior in high school takes a jagged path through my mind. I got in, and some of the other kids even praised me, only to have Aunt Clara shoot down my accomplishment when I told her. I had been so certain she'd finally be proud of me. But no. Frivolous activities wouldn't get me a decent job once I graduated high school. Whenever I mentioned college as a good way of reaching that goal, she dismissed that possibility too. According to Aunt Clara, college was not required to work the till in a store. I remained in the glee club, defiant and upset, and managed to do so until the day I couldn't take it anymore and left East Quay.

Now the girls sing a stunning rendition of "Fade Away," which I feel stupid for not recognizing as one of the biggest hits of the summer. I can tell the girls are a little uncertain as they change key, but they hold their own, even without a conductor. If they're this good without one, they must really shine when their leader is present.

"Your turn, Romi, was it?" The waitress taps me on the shoulder. I flinch and see the stage is empty. "Do you have any sheet music for the accompanist?" She nods to the man at the piano.

"No. I mean, I sing a cappella." I rub my palms against my thighs.

"All right. On you go." The waitress gives me a quick smile.

The room is lit only by the small lanterns sitting on each table. I can't make out anybody but the faces of the patrons closest to the stage, and that's a good thing. I can just sing and pretend I'm in the subway as usual.

"Hi. My name is Romi and I'm going to sing 'Never Enough' from *The Greatest Showman*." Musical numbers usually do well, and this song means a lot to me. I haven't seen the movie, but after listening to the recording at the library in New York many times, I know it well. I never dwell on why, exactly, a certain song speaks to me. It just does.

I grip the microphone hard but leave it in its stand while inhaling deeply. As I start to sing, I know it's going to be an all-right performance. I don't add any of the interaction that's necessary sometimes in the subway. That'd be awkward among this crowd. As I let the song build, I'm grateful for the excellent sound system. Reaching the crescendo and then the soft ending of the song, I can only hope that I'm not the only lover of musicals in Westport today.

There's a moment of silence, and then the members of the audience applaud and shout in appreciation. Stunned, I stand there, suddenly at a loss how to get down from the stage. Hell. I don't even know how to let go of the microphone. Eventually, the applause dies down and I take a bow, knowing how important it is to be polite. If anyone here is about to hand me some cash, I can't come off as an asshole.

The boy with the standup comedy act does well, and people shout his name. No doubt he's locally known. In a town this size, most people are, probably.

"Romi!" Stephanie and Lisa show up at my side. "You were amazing! You can *sing*!"

"Thank you." I have to smile at the exuberant teenagers. "Your choir did a great job, and when you consider the fact you had no conductor, it was even better."

"You think so? We almost had a disaster at the key change. I hope Giselle didn't faint. She's extremely sensitive to such things." Stephanie crinkles her nose, but her eyes show no real concern. "If anyone sounds pitchy, I swear she breaks into hives."

"So true. Why don't you and your new friend come sit at the table? We've ordered calamari for the entire table and have seats to spare." Appearing as if out of nowhere, Tierney shows up next to us. "And I can promise you that neither the choir nor you, Ms…?"

"Just Romi." I place my twitchy hands on my back, holding on tight.

"Romi. You were a welcome surprise. Won't you join us?" Tierney regards me with friendly curiosity. "And neither of you was pitchy enough to cause my wife a bout of the hives."

A free meal? Is she kidding? "Thank you. I'd love to… um…?" What was her last name? Something hyphenated?

"Just Tierney will do, Romi." Tierney grins. "I see the other choir members are joining their families. Come along."

I obediently walk behind the other three as we make our way to the table by the emergency exit. It's a large, round table, able to seat eight people. Four of the seats are taken already.

"Romi, let me introduce you really quick." Tierney motions to the blond woman that has a black retriever sitting close to her. "This is my wife, Giselle. And that's Charley." She points at the dog. "You can pat her if Giselle says it's okay. Giselle, this is Romi."

"It's okay," Giselle says, raising an eyebrow at Tierney as she extends her hand to me. Her sonorous voice, combined with her classic beauty, makes my mouth go dry, but I take her hand. In a way she reminds me of Gail.

"Nice to meet you, Giselle." I have an odd feeling that she's someone familiar, but that's of course impossible.

"Okay. This lovely lady is Manon Belmont. You may have heard of the Belmont Foundation," Tierney says and smiles at the woman on Giselle's other side. With chocolate-brown hair and even, slate-gray eyes, she seems…untouchable, somehow. Still, there's nothing standoffish about her. Manon just looks like she constantly assesses her surroundings, including its people.

"Hello, Romi." Manon shakes my hand before indicating the woman next to her. "This is Eryn, my wife."

I'm greeted by a vigorous handshake as Eryn leans over the table, her long, red braid dangling dangerously close to the large plate of calamari.

"Have a seat, please, and tell us about yourself." Tierney motioned for the chair between Lisa and Eryn. "We're always curious about new faces—especially when said face can sing."

She winks at me, but my panic is rising from a level three to at least a seven.

"Nothing much to tell. I'm new around here, staying in the rural area of East Quay," I say, hoping I sound casual enough. "I saw a poster about the open mic here. That's about it."

Stephanie leans past Lisa. "Nah-uh. You sing like a pro. There must be more to your story."

"Stephanie." Giselle's tone is light, but it holds a soft warning. "Let Romi decide what she wants to share."

"Sure. Absolutely." Stephanie doesn't appear to mind the discreet correction. "I just think you're amazing, Romi."

"Thank you." I look longingly at the plate and have to push my hands in between my thighs to not grab a fork and shuffle all that deep-fried goodness into my mouth.

"Why don't we dig in before it gets cold?" Manon says, and I wonder if she's read my mind.

"Yay! Calamari," Lisa says. "Haven't had Italian since the last time I was here. Corazon makes the best Mexican food, but variety is good, right?" She elbows me gently. Lisa is short, a little chubby, and very cute with her black ringlets falling down her back.

"Who is Corazon?" I ask as I force myself to take just one piece of the calamari at a time, dip it in my own little bowl of dressing, and chew it with so much gratitude I could cry.

"My foster mom. She's awesome." Lisa grins and spears a new piece from the large plate.

"Sounds fantastic." I swallow hard. It does. I've never been in the system, and for a long time I was told I needed to be grateful that I had a relative willing to care for me. Seeing Lisa beam as she talks about her foster mom reinforces the feeling I had growing up. Foster care might have been better. Perhaps.

The conversation decreases a little as we all eat. The waiter shows up next to Tierney. "Will there be seven for the main course, Ms. Edwards-Bonnaire?"

"Geez, Phil. Don't go all nuts with the surnames. We come

here all the time, and we've told you every time that you should use our first names. It's confusing when we're sharing last names left and right."

"Very well. Tierney," Phil says, looking pained at the clearly frivolous suggestion.

"And yes. There will be seven of us. May we have the menus back?"

Phil has clearly anticipated the request and hands them over to us. My eyes roam the many choices of Italian food. If you're treated to a meal, nothing's better than Italian. It fills you up, and the feeling of being full can last almost twenty-four hours. Not tonight, though. These women seem really observant, and if I eat as if I haven't seen real food in weeks, which is kind of true, they'll get suspicious. At least that's what my panic-infused mind tells me.

"Now, Romi, choose whatever you like. No silliness about going for the cheapest alternative." As if knowing more than she should, Eryn winks at me over her menu. "I know that's what I used to do when Manon first started taking me out on dates. We used to go to fancy places, and I couldn't afford to split the check—so I'd order a salad or an appetizer. Don't even think about that now."

I blush. I can feel the heat in my cheeks, and I honestly contemplate slipping off the chair and hiding under the table. "Thank you," I murmur, not knowing where to look.

"Eryn is a bit too straightforward sometimes," Manon says calmly, "but she's right. I can understand being invited to have dinner can feel awkward when it's out of the blue. Trust me, we do this all the time with different choir members and others. It's no big deal."

All right. Since they insist. I look up the dish that seems most plentiful rather than expensive or fancy, and it turns out to be a huge pasta dish. My stomach will no doubt rebel tonight or tomorrow, but I can't resist it.

I eat in silence, listening absentmindedly to the conversation among the other women and girls. Then there's a lull, no, a dead quiet, and I realize six pairs of eyes are looking at me expectantly. Seven, counting Charley the dog.

"Sorry," I murmur and place my fork and spoon on the side of the almost-empty plate.

"Hey. No need. I'm glad you're enjoying the food," Tierney says. "We asked if you want to join the choir. It would be as a junior choir leader. Part-time. With a salary, of course."

I stare at her and then look around the table at the other six. "Wh-what?"

"I know it's sudden, but you may have heard back at the office area that Carrie, the girls' regular leader, had to cancel?" Tierney leans forward on her elbows. "Carrie's great, but she's dealing with...stuff. We need someone to fill in for her and assist her when need be."

"But I haven't been in a choir in years." I blink hard. This must be a mistake. There's no way I can do this, and that fact hurts so much, I dig my nails into my thighs to keep from screaming. A paying job, just within my reach, and I can't accept it.

"Your musicality is obvious, and you'll learn the ropes from Carrie." Manon folds her napkin after delicately dabbing at her lips. "As Tierney said, it's not a full-time position, but approximately eighteen hours a week, which could amount to more when the choir starts entering competitions and so on." She smiles at Stephanie and Lisa, who both wriggle happily on their chairs.

"Please, Romi. You'd fit in perfectly. How old are you, by the way?" Lisa beams at me.

"Twenty-two," I say absentmindedly and think I see surprise in the women's eyes.

"Even better. I figured you as a senior in high school or a college freshman perhaps." Manon nodded approvingly. "Why don't you come to my home office in East Quay tomorrow afternoon, and we'll talk more? In the meantime, think of this as a TA position in college."

I have no knowledge of college life, let alone what a TA does and if they're paid. How can I refuse? Perhaps I can tell this woman, when it's only us, face-to-face, some of the truth, and she'll realize why I'm not such a good fit. It stings when I see Lisa's and Stephanie's hopeful faces, but I can't change the facts about myself, about my situation. "Just give me the address and I'll be there." I force a smile, and for a moment, Manon's eyes show nothing but compassion in an oddly knowing way. Perhaps she really *is* clairvoyant or something.

After we've managed to have some gelato for dessert, the girls are moaning about not being able to ever move again.

"I hear you. Let me get the Jeep. We'll drop Romi off at her house on the way back to East Quay." Tierney jumps up as if she hasn't had a three-course meal and a large cappuccino. "You okay?" she asks Giselle, who merely nods.

Manon walks out with her, and I assume she's getting her car as well.

I'm torn. Again. I've dreaded walking in the dark as it's now nine p.m., but how can I let them give me a lift without raising suspicion? Then I think of that gravel road about three hundred yards south of Gail's property. It leads into some dense woods and shrubbery, where I can hope they don't know that only an old abandoned cottage stands.

Tierney calls Giselle's cell and lets us know she and Manon have pulled up. As we leave the restaurant, Eryn places a gentle hand on my back. I flinch but try to mask my reaction by coughing, a trick I've had to resort to many times.

"It was lovely to meet you, Romi," Eryn says. "I won't be at the house tomorrow, but do give Manon's offer some serious thought. She's a true problem solver, and no matter what may come up, she'll find a way to work around it. Trust me."

Oddly, I'm inclined to trust her for a few seconds, but my life experience has showed me how futile that is. Yet this time, I really, really want to believe these women, these girls. They've accepted me, at least for tonight, and been nothing but kind and generous. "Thank you, Eryn. I appreciate the offer more than I can say, but…" I shrug, helpless about how to explain. "And thank you for the meal. You have no idea how wonderful it was for me." Now, that's enough. I can't share more than that. Danger, danger.

I get into the back seat of the spacious Jeep next to Lisa and Stephanie. The girls are giggling about something I'm not really listening to. The two women in the front talk in quieter voices, but even if I don't hear the words, I can feel the affection, the love, between them. I know better than to indulge in a fantasy of belonging with someone, a person, a family, but I come damn close in that Jeep, heading for a gravel road that leads to nowhere.

CHAPTER FIVE

Gail

The late fall air is crisp. It almost hurts to inhale it where I sit on the stairs of my back porch with a blanket around my shoulders. I have closed the door behind me to not let the light from the living room pollute the darkness that is lit only by stars and a receding moon. I'm still cross with myself for my moment of weakness earlier. I hate tears, mainly my own, as they make me feel so damn vulnerable. I cannot allow that, not even now when I've lost...well, pretty much everything. It serves me right to sit out here in the chilly night, looking at a desolate fragment of a moon surrounded by stars so far away from it, they're not truly part of the same sky.

Talking to Neill, and I know I should call him back, was not what I needed today. I can't handle sympathy and certainly not all the practical suggestions he gave me. They grate on my nerves, and if I were at all like my violin, I would scrape off the hairs on the bow. I'm all thorns, and it's no big surprise that my peers, and those I used to call friends, are recoiling. I don't like being around me either, but I have little choice.

At a distance, I see a car pass, and as it lights up the outlines of the bushes in the garden, I, again, question what the hell I'm doing out here in the sticks. What was I thinking when I opted for this well-kept, but horribly decorated, house in between a field and a forest? I knew so little of this part of Rhode Island before I came. I thought it consisted of mainly quaint fishing villages and posh houses belonging to summer guests. I wasn't aware it had so many farms, fields, and forests. Of course, I had to buy the sorriest-looking house. Perhaps I need to list it again and buy something in the Caribbean? I snort. Hardly. I'd go mad in such a climate. There's no way an East Coast native like me would ever feel at ease among palm trees, lagoons, flashy hotels, and whatnot. No, I might as well sulk here in the cold.

A faint sound from the garden makes me go rigid. An animal? I've seen plenty of deer, wild turkeys, and a god-awful lot of squirrels and chipmunks around here. This sounds bigger though. I spot a faint light and press back against the step behind me. Who the hell is trespassing, and what do they think they'll find if they intend to break in?

A diminutive figure, not terribly imposing, enters slowly between the bushes. It stops, then moves out from the shadows, and the moon lights up a face that thankfully is familiar.

"Can you explain why you're trespassing through my yard at this time in the evening?" I know I startle the girl. What was her name? Romi. Yes. Serves her right for scaring me.

"Oh, God." Romi squeaks and stops.

"Yes? I'm waiting for an explanation." I stand up. "You on your way home?" I try to remember in which direction she lives but have to confess I don't recall.

"Yes." Romi steps closer. "I'm sorry. I was taking a shortcut as it's so cold."

I can see she's shivering. "Oh, for heaven's sake. If you can help me with something, you can come in for some hot tea." Hey. Where did that come from? Perhaps I'm channeling the chill inside me, but it's true that I need to move a box my cleaners forgot that blocks the entrance to the family-size bathroom on the second floor. I can't do it with one hand.

"Sure." Romi steps closer yet, and I can clearly see the

expression in her hazel eyes. She has a wild, apprehensive look, and she's keeping her lower lip firmly in place between her teeth.

"Come on then. Take your shoes off." I step back through the porch door, holding it open for Romi. She stops just inside and kicks off sneakers that have seen better days. Now that I watch her in lamplight, I can tell she's still shaking.

"Am I that frightening?" I ask casually and point in the direction of the kitchen. "Tea first. Box of books later."

"I really don't want to disturb you this late," Romi says quietly. "I can come back tomorrow morning and help you with whatever you need."

"Now there's a thought. If you manage to shove the box away from my bathroom door, then you can perhaps help me put the books up in the bedroom bookshelf tomorrow." I walk over and set the electric kettle to boil some water. "I'll pay you, of course."

"Oh, there's no need—"

"Nonsense. I don't know about what you're used to, but I don't pull young ladies off the lawn and make them work for free." I frown at her, but to my surprise, she smiles faintly. Huh.

"Somehow I think people are easily persuaded to do your bidding, should you need them to." Romi accepts the mug I give her. The tea-bag string dangles on the side, and she looks at the mug with the strangest expression.

"I know. Garish color choices, right?" I cradle my own version of the brightly colored mug. "They hold the temperature for a long time though."

"Yes." Romi plays with the string. "I apologize."

"For trespassing? Don't worry. As long as it's you and not some gang set on a home invasion, I don't mind. It's not like I have priceless rosebushes to tend to."

"No, for saying that about people eager to do your bidding. That was rude." Romi pulls out the tea bag and wraps it around a spoon. Without prompting she unwinds it and gets up and throws it into the trash. Sitting down, she sips the tea carefully.

"It was rather funny. And I admit, it used to be true." I must be desperate for companionship as it seems so damn easy to talk to this girl.

"Used to be?" Romi tilts her head and pushes her surplus-looking jacket off. She's dressed all in black, and now she somehow seems a little older.

"Before this." I raise my arm in its orthosis.

"That doesn't make sense." Romi frowns. "Why would injuring your arm change things so much...I mean, in how people see you?"

"Oh, trust me. It did. Sometimes because of other people, sometimes because of me." I hadn't accepted that truth before. I shrug with the shoulder belonging to my good arm. "Worst of all was the pity from my peers because my career as a musician was over."

"You were a musician? What instrument?" Romi's expression is kind, but not pitying at all. That's the only reason I don't bite her head off.

"Violinist." I raise my chin, challenging her to say something trite.

"I'm sorry you were hurt, either way." Romi holds her hands protectively around the ugly mug.

"Thank you." A bit taken aback at the lack of the usual gushing attempts to comfort me for losing everything that mattered in my life, I lean back in the kitchen chair. "What about you? I haven't seen you in a few days. I sometimes see you pass out on the road, but you disappear just as quickly."

Romi's cheeks go pink. "I've, um, been looking for work. I walk into Westport and use the computer in the library." She traces the pattern of a flower-filled barrel on her mug.

"What kind of work?" I ask, curious now. This conversation has certainly stopped my day from being mundane. And lonely.

"Anything really. Nothing too elaborate though. Busgirl. Cleaner. That sort of thing."

I get the feeling this girl has more potential than that, but clearly, she doesn't think so. "Or lifting boxes," I say softly, and she winces.

"Nothing wrong with that." She has steel in her voice now.

"Certainly not, if that makes you content." I could never imagine that cleaning or moving other people's possessions would bring anyone true fulfillment, but I'm not stupid. I know that for many people, finding any sort of honest work is a struggle.

"Content?" Romi seems to taste the word, as if it's alien to her. "Yes, maybe."

"If you truly are looking for work, I can offer you some. I have a basement that needs sorting and clearing out."

Romi pales and lets go of her mug so fast, she spills a few drops. "Your basement?"

"Yes. The previous owner left the house as it is now, full of furniture, decorations, and all her belongings. Even old photo albums."

Romi stands. "I see. Well, thank you. I accept. Can I move the box now, before it gets too late?" Looking vulnerable, she shows tension in her big hazel eyes.

"Certainly." I motion for her to ascend the stairs at the far end of the kitchen. She takes the steps in twos, skipping lithely up the staircase. I walk up in a slower pace, as I'm afraid of bumping my arm against the wall next to this narrow staircase.

When I reach the next floor, Romi has already pushed the crate a few yards. She must have figured out which is the master bedroom already. Soon, it sits inside the door where I won't trip over it.

"Thank you," I say briskly. "Tomorrow morning, you can put the books up in alphabetical order for me."

She looks hesitant, and I think she's going to decline helping after all. "Hmm. That. Or, since you're going to have them in your bedroom, you could have them color coded." Romi seems calmer now, cocking her head.

"Color coded?" I frown. "What kind of system is that?"

"It's feng shui." Romi gestures toward the empty bookshelves.

"Dear God." I really don't have time or the affinity for new-age drivel. "How do you suppose I'll be able to find anything?"

"It'll be very restful for your eyes, and that means you'll sleep better." Romi looks down at the rug, and when I follow her glance, she places one foot on top of the other, but I can still see the hole in her threadbare left sock. "And they can still be in alphabetical order within each color category."

"Where have you learned this?" I don't find myself surprised often, but this girl, no, young woman, manages to effortlessly astonish me.

"At the library." Smiling wanly, Romi places her hands on her back.

"How old are you?" I ask.

"Twenty-two," she says, and I'm starting to think I can't read people at all. Sure, she has a quiet maturity, but I thought she was younger.

"And you?" Romi says, raising her chin in a subtle challenge.

"Thirty-six." I shrug. Age is immaterial.

"So, feng shui, or old school?" Now Romi's eyes sparkle, and I find myself staring at them as if I haven't really noticed how unique they are before now. Hazel, yes, but now they glimmer like rose gold in the muted light of the bedside lamps.

"Let me think about that," I say, though dead certain there will be no color coding.

"I should get home." Romi inches toward the door, the sparkles in her eyes fading. "It's getting late."

"Of course. I'll write you a check when you come by tomorrow."

She stops and slowly turns toward me. Where the sparkles enticed me only moments ago, I see now only dark shadows, emphasized by her dark makeup. "A check?" Romi's shoulders slump forward, and she wipes her hands on her pants. "Any possibility you can pay me in cash?"

This gives me pause. A threadbare young woman asking to be paid in cash. That sends up warning flags, and I'm seconds from saying I've changed my mind, when the slightest quiver of her lower lip catches my eye. Sure, she pulls it in quickly between her teeth, something I recognize from earlier, in the backyard. "Why not, if that's more convenient for you. We do live out in the sticks, and you seem to get around by walking for the most part. Closest bank is in East Quay, I understand, or in Westport, as we're right on the border."

"Yes," Romi murmurs. "That's right."

"Well, I'll get cash ready for you. I'm driving into East Quay tomorrow anyway." The sane part of me wants to make sure she realizes I don't keep cash at the house. Better safe and so on.

Her relief is palpable, and I know there's a story there. What yet again surprises me is that Romi's story interests me. At all. For the first time since the accident I've raised my eyes off the ground and looked at someone else. Hell, not only since the accident. I've been self-absorbed for many years and lived only for my music. This is why I deserve to be secluded in an ugly farmhouse in the middle of nowhere.

I walk Romi to the porch door, watch her don her worn sneakers. "You sure you're okay walking home alone?" I know I sound annoyed rather than concerned.

"I'll be fine. It's, um, not far." Romi fidgets and walks down the few steps to the yard. "See you tomorrow. Nine? Ten?"

"Nine is fine, if you're up."

"I'll be here." Romi nods and disappears around the corner and into the dark.

I close the porch door and turn the deadbolt. I wonder where Romi lives and if she's on her own. Surely if she has a parent, or anyone else looking out for her, they'd make sure she had some decent clothes. Rubbing the back of my neck with my good hand,

I walk through the rooms downstairs and turn off the lights. As I switch them off in the living room, I think I see a quick, soft light at the other end of the house, but when I get closer to the windows, it's only the same moonlit yard I studied before.

I walk upstairs and into the bathroom. A bath might help me relax, even if I must admit that I'm not as tense as I was before Romi showed up. I see no significance in this occurrence, as I regard it as a coincidence, merely thinking that I might sleep more than one hour at a time this night.

There's always hope.

CHAPTER SIX

Romi

Standing in the basement, boots in hand, having entered through Gail's house rather than the cellar door, I try to look impressed. "That's quite the collection of preserves." I motion toward the vast number of glass jars on the shelves.

"And then some." Gail rests her hip against the table where I sat so many times when I was little and wrote on the labels for my aunt. "You were so damned fast sorting the books upstairs. If you don't mind, I want you to go through all the jars—look at the dates and examine the seals. If they're all right, I'll donate them to a shelter. Those that are too old or damaged, I'll have someone come collect them." She points to a free area on the floor next to the door leading to the yard. "You can put them there."

"Okay." I'm tongue-tied and rattled, being here in the basement with Gail, so close to the shelf that leads to the secret room. She's no fool, this woman. To the contrary. I don't think I've seen anyone look at me like Gail does, scrutinizing, calculating, and, very briefly, perhaps twice, with stunned curiosity. One of those times was when I persuaded her to try the feng shui approach with her book collection. I'm sure she intended to go old school, authors in alphabetical order. It was pretty funny when she stared at the much more restful look of color coordination.

"When you're done, that's it for today. I've picked up a few of those jars, and they're damn heavy. I don't want you to overdo." Gail tilts her head as she regards me. "I'm driving into East Quay half past twelve. You think you'll be done by then?"

"Sure thing. It won't take long." I swallow. "Um. Can I hitch a ride? I was going into town myself in the afternoon." Where I get the courage to ask, I don't know, but I'm sure I'm pushing it. Why would she ever do such a thing?

"Why not?" Gail shrugs, lifting only her left shoulder. Her injured arm is tucked into its orthosis and also in a sling today. She moves as if she wants to cradle it like a baby, but of course she wouldn't do something like that in front of anyone else. I don't like to show anything I perceive as a weakness either. "If you want to wash up before we go, you can do that in the guest bathroom on the first floor. Second door to the left. And don't dawdle."

"I won't. Thanks." I feel myself smile in a way I'm not used to, my mouth wide and open.

Gail blinks. "Hmm. No problem. I'll be upstairs in my study. Don't disturb me unless you absolutely can't figure out something. I can't imagine whatever could be among these… items." She doesn't wait for me to acknowledge her words before going upstairs.

I'm glad Gail's going to the study rather than the spy corner in the living room. I know I'm getting my hands on some cash through helping her, and perhaps whatever Manon Belmont has up her sleeve will pan out in a good way, but I still need to harvest some of the jars. I won't take any of the ones Gail wants to donate. I just couldn't, but if I see any that are one month too old, that wouldn't be as bad a theft, would it? I try to convince myself of that theory.

To not *dawdle*—I mean, who uses words like that—I hurry over to the shelf farthest from the door. I sort through all the pickled cucumbers first and have to concede that most of them are too old. Six are still okay and intact, and one I place over by the swing shelf. Then I fear Gail may come down unexpectedly and see me create a stack she didn't give instructions about and move them closer to the ones by the door.

Applesauce has fared best among all the jars. Twenty of them to donate, four to me, and the rest will need to be thrown out. I inspect the red peppers, apricots, orange marmalade, and even some homemade sauerkraut. I decide on approximately the same ratio for all of them.

My back starts to hurt when I haul the largest ones over to the door. I place them out of the way so I can still get in without risking running into any of them. That could make a big mess.

I glance at the ceiling. I can't hear a thing from upstairs. Hurrying over to the swing shelf, I open it faster than usual now that I don't have to be afraid of Gail hearing noises from below. I carry the jars I put aside for me down the few steps. I can't slow down even if I'm afraid I'll stumble and send some of the jars crashing onto the floor below. Every time I return for two more jars, I listen for footsteps, for creaking floorboards, or for Gail's voice. Still nothing. Holding the last two jars, one under each arm, I almost skip all the steps in one jump, and just as I'm about to put them on the small table, I hear her. I toss them onto the bed, rush up the four steps, swivel, and push the swing shelf closed. Not about to wait for Gail to stand in front of that particular shelf and draw her attention to it, I throw myself down next to the discarded batch of jars, but I slip on the part of the concrete floor that has been polished smooth by many feet over many years. I careen toward the jars and hold my hands out to try and stop myself, but I still make a lot of noise as I slam into them.

Pain shoots up through my hands and arms, and my right hip smarts so badly, tears form in my eyes.

"Romi!" Gail sounds upset, and soon she crouches next to me, her good hand on my shoulder. "What happened?"

"I slipped." I meant to say I slipped carrying the last of the jars, but my hip is still making my tears well up, and I'm trying to contain myself.

"I can tell. I saw you just after you went down, but I heard you do it. Are you all right?" Gail's voice is unsteady too. "Let me see your hands."

"No. Hands are okay," I lie. "My hip took the brunt of it." I look at the jars, trying to stealthily blink the tears away. They all look whole.

"As long as you didn't cut yourself." Gail cups my chin and studies me. The touch is warm, no, hot to my skin. I forget to breathe for a second. "Can you stand?" she asks, letting go.

"Sure." I move to stand on my knees, which I'm glad I didn't slam into the concrete. "I'm such a klutz."

"I wouldn't know, but I'm glad you didn't hit your head. You didn't, did you?" Gail lifts her hand as if she means to feel through my hair for bumps but lowers it again.

"Eh, no. Just my hip, really." I watch her rise with enviable grace, injured arm or not.

"Go upstairs and clean up. Examine your hip and make sure you didn't break the skin." Motioning for me to walk ahead of her, Gail sends a quick glance toward the shelves and then follows me. "I can tell you managed to save quite a few for me to donate. Good."

"Yes, about a third, almost." I kick off my old boots after I get upstairs. Then I remember that I'm not supposed to know the layout of the house. "Second door to the left, you said?"

"Correct. I'll be in my study until we leave." Gail checks the time. "In half an hour. Actually, it's a good thing you're going with me. We can stop at the ATM so I can get your cash."

My cheeks burn. Why is that? I did a job for her, last night, though tiny, and today. Why do I feel so awkward taking her money? I walk into the guest bathroom. It's a smaller bathroom that boasts a shower, sink, and toilet. I use the latter, and when I'm done, I examine my hip before I pull my pants up. It's going to get black and blue as all hell. Damn. But no broken skin, at least. I pull off my shirt and the worn tank top. They were clean this morning, and sniffing them, I think they're okay still. I wash under my arms and then my face. Taking one of the towels I press it to my face, only to moan when I feel how thick and soft it is. My towels in the secret room aren't bad, but before I came back here, I had to make do with coarse paper towels or scratchy, cheap, terry-cloth washcloths. These are amazing.

I raise my eyes to look at myself in the mirror. I'm pale, I mean, when am I not, but there's more. Something new and different. And painful. It dawns on me. I know now why taking money from Gail for a job I've done makes bile rise in my throat. I cling to the sink and know what I see reflected in the mirror as I stare at myself.

Utter, overwhelming, and mind-blowing guilt.

Gail

Following the head waitress, I weave through the tables among the lunch guests at the Sea Stone Café. According to its website, I have entered the new wing, a restaurant to complement the original café. Rustic, with that special New England charm, so common still in interior design, it seems very popular, considering very few tables are empty. I battle an unwelcome feeling of vulnerability as I'm directed to a window table overlooking the marina. After ordering a house-blend coffee, receiving the menu, and, oh, yes, let's not forget, answering the polite question, "Just one of you, then, ma'am," I focus on the view.

Only five boats are still in the water by the docks. I watch them move as the gentle waves rock the boats between the fenders. If I were prone to being easily hypnotized, I could fall into a trance.

Another waitress breaks me out of my reverie as she arrives with my coffee. I appreciate that she's quick, as I already know that I want clam chowder and bread. The woman nods and smiles warmly at me before removing the menu. I direct my attention back to the window after she leaves, not sure why I thought having lunch alone was a great idea to begin with. Yes, I'm fed up with the frozen dinners at the house. I've tried cooking using just one hand, but even opening cans is a problem. I'll have to get one of those electric openers at this rate.

The haunting thoughts of my injured arm nearly drive my appetite out the window. During a few weeks after the first surgery, depression hit so badly I could barely swallow any type of food. I lost more than twenty pounds, and, sure, I've regained most of it, but after that experience, the idea of losing my appetite frightens me. Normally I truly do appreciate food, but I also need to stay well-nourished to be able to heal.

The chowder appears before me, along with steaming warm slices of bread. I realize it might become a bit of a chore to put butter on it.

"Do you need help holding the plate of butter, ma'am?" the waitress asks in a low voice. I cringe but tell myself it could be worse. She could've offered to butter it for me.

"Yes. Thank you," I say, forcing myself to not snap at the kind woman.

She places two fingers at the edge of the plate, and I manage to spread some butter onto the bread. I'm relieved to feel my mouth water at the sight of the thick slices. So, no risk of not being able to eat just yet.

The waitress leaves without saying anything more, and I decide to tip her well.

As I begin to eat, my mind shifts from boats and kind waitresses to Romi. Before driving down to the marina, I dropped her off in the northern part of East Quay, which is clearly a wealthier area. I admit I'm curious who she might know there, since it's obvious that Romi comes from another income bracket.

When I stopped at the drive-in ATM and withdrew the money I owed her from last night and this morning, she simply stared at the bills in her hands.

"That's too much," she said, frowning. "I only worked for a few hours."

This, somehow, made me angry. Not at her per se, but at how little she seemed to value herself. "You worked hard with those gigantic jars. You did what I asked you to do, quickly and efficiently. Just take what I owe you, and that's that."

Romi pressed her small frame against the door, her eyes huge. "All right. Thank you." Swallowing visibly, she folded the bills and tucked them into the inner pocket of her military-style jacket.

During our drive into East Quay, she hadn't said a word, which suited me fine, but now her unsettled look made her silence less comfortable. "Where can I drop you off?"

Romi pulled a very small notebook from her pocket and flipped open a page. "At the top of Main Street will be fine, thank you." She tucked the notebook back into her pocket and put her hands between her knees.

So I did.

Driving an automatic is easier for me, but it's still awkward to put the gear shift into drive or reverse with my left hand. I make do, and as I pulled over where Main Street ends and divides into three smaller roads, Romi turned and looked at me with something unreadable in her eyes. If I hadn't known any better, I would have guessed it was remorse, but that was of course ridiculous.

Now as I eat the last of my chowder and reach for another slice of bread, I'm not so sure. I'm also uncertain why I bother with these musings. I don't know this young woman. She's my neighbor, she passes my house sometimes, and…and she looks like she's all alone, something I have no way of knowing, of course. Perhaps that sense of being isolated, whether voluntarily or not, is the common thread that makes my mind return to her so often? That, and curiosity, I must admit. I was always a sucker for a puzzle or any type of mystery, and I can swear Romi has a story.

My mother used to tell anyone who would listen that I was hopeless to watch crime shows with on TV, as I always guessed whodunit halfway into the show or movie. I could tell she was secretly proud, though. And she also insisted that it was my way of directing all my attention to a single subject that made me into the musician I later became. Is that why I'm drifting now, emotionally? I have no purpose and nothing to focus on except Romi, the enigma.

My cell phone vibrates in my left jacket pocket. I glance around and see that the closest patrons around me have left and I won't disturb anyone if I take the call. Looking at the screen, I see it's Neill. I click the green receiver icon. "I apologize for biting your head off, Neill," I say in lieu of hello.

A few moments of silence and then he chuckles warmly. "Weighed on your mind, did it, girl? Don't worry about it. Already forgotten."

I exhale. "Thank you. I can be such a bitch."

"Cut yourself some slack. I was treading where your vulnerability lives and thrives, and you weren't ready for it. I can be such a busybody." Neill's warm voice wraps around me, and I know I'm very lucky to have a friend who understands so much, and cares even more.

"Thank you." I know I'm infamous for foregoing niceties more often than not, but with Neill, the man who has seen me through both good times and bad, I find it easy to express gratitude. It dawns on me that I've thanked Romi on several occasions but push the thought aside. "So, what's up?"

"I was wondering if you'd like some guests over the week-end. Laurence and I feel like a little road trip, and he's curious about your farmhouse. I've tried to tell him you don't have a barn or cows, but he thinks he can at least persuade you to get a goat."

I snort. "A goat?" Laurence has been engaged to Neill for more than a decade, and the two men's well-developed, silly sense of humor always amazes me. "If he moves in and takes care of the critter, why not?"

Neill guffaws, and I know it's not so much what I said that makes him laugh, but the fact that I'm in the mood to joke around.

It's rare these days, but when it happens, it's exclusively because of Neill and Laurence.

We chat on about nothing much at all, but I decide that I really would love their company. "Today's Wednesday." I smile as I sign the receipt, adding a generous tip for the waitress. "Why don't you drive up Friday after work, and we'll have all of Saturday and most of Sunday?"

"Brilliant!" A slapping sound tells me Neill has smacked his palm on his desk, which lets me know he's really happy. He can give an entire lecture on the direct correlation of happiness and slapping furniture. If he does that with Laurence present, his fiancé will go off on a tangent where stinging palms can have naughtier reasons. That's where I usually stop them since I hate blushing, and they'll make me go crimson with the double entendres if I don't reel them in.

We hang up and I rise. Placing my coat around my shoulders with a well-practiced movement, I walk toward the entrance. As I round the head waitress station and reach for the door, another, half-hidden door opens, and two women step outside. I automatically cast a quick glance their way and stop, midstride. A curvaceous, stunning blond woman in her mid-fifties, perhaps, and a younger, tall and wiry woman with black, short hair. The latter is vaguely familiar, but the first one I'd recognize anywhere.

"Vivian Harding?" I say hesitantly, because running into the world-renowned mezzo-soprano here of all places is far too unexpected.

"Yes?" the blond woman, who is indeed who I think she is, says and turns toward me. Her eyes don't meet mine, and I remember reading that she lost her sight some years ago.

"It's Gail Owen, if you remember." I suddenly regret starting this conversation. "We've worked together on several occasions."

"Gail?" Vivian's cautious smile turns brilliant. "What on earth? Mike, this is Gail Owen, violin virtuoso, whom I've known since she was second violin in the Boston Philharmonic.

And this gorgeous woman is my wife, Michaela Stone, but she prefers Mike."

Vivian extends her hand too far to the right of me.

"Ms. Owen has her right arm in a sling, Vivian," Mike says kindly, then nods toward me. "Nice to meet you."

Without missing a beat, Vivian reaches out with her left hand instead. I take it and squeeze it gently.

"So nice to run in to both of you," I say, not sure what to feel right now. "And unexpected."

"I'll say." Vivian gives one of her famous, raucous laughs. "But a treat nonetheless. Are you coming or going?"

"Going, actually. Just had a lovely clam chowder."

"That makes me happy to hear," Mike says. "This is my place, even if I'm not part of the day-to-day work anymore." She towers over both Vivian and me, and dressed mostly in black, she's a formidable sight. So, Vivian married this much-younger woman. I try to remember if I've read about it, but to be honest, the last ten years before the accident, I was touring the entire world nonstop, and afterward, I haven't been able to muster any interest in news or gossip. When it comes to the music world, I vaguely remember Vivian working with an improv group. Perhaps Mike is part of that?

"We should meet up, Gail. So much has happened since we last worked together." Vivian waves the hand that isn't tucked under Mike's arm. "We're having that dinner party on Friday. You must come. I want to know all about—"

"I'm sorry, Vivian. I'm having visitors from out of town." Part of me is sad to miss it, but for the most part, I'm relieved.

"They have to come too!" Vivian laughs again, and who can resist this force of nature? "How many of you can I expect?"

Neill and Laurence will never forgive me if I keep them from meeting Vivian Harding. I'm trapped, and I know it. "Three. This is very generous, Vivian." I put on my best smile for Mike's sake.

"Nonsense!" Vivian pulls a cell phone from her purse.

"Contacts. New. Name. Gail Owen. Cell-phone number." She holds it up to me, nodding encouragingly.

Taken aback, I give my number and the phone beeps.

"Excellent. Text Gail Owen." Vivian gives an address and ends with, "Friday, seven p.m., casual attire."

It's my cell's turn to beep.

"Well, we better go have our belated lunch after all the exercise we just got in the basement," Vivian says, beaming.

I gawk. I can't help it. This makes Mike laugh. "Vivian, you have to stop doing that. You're embarrassing Gail." Taking pity on me, Mike places a hand on my left arm for a moment. "We have a music studio below, and we've been rehearsing."

Ah. Thank God. "I see. Well, then you deserve to eat in peace. See you Friday." I want to escape so badly now and process this turn of events that I'm already halfway out the door.

"We look forward to it," Vivian says and waves in my general direction. Mike does the same, and I'm free to go.

How the hell did I end up in this situation? Yes, the guys will love it, but I'll be the one having to suffer through questions about my arm, my destroyed career—no, my destroyed *life*.

CHAPTER SEVEN

Romi

Manon's house is huge. I've seen these types of houses from a pavement distance, of course, but never been close to one, let alone inside. I let my hand hover over the button next to the massive door, but then press it for a few seconds. It's barely audible from where I'm standing. I take a few steps back, certain that it's not polite to stand close enough for the person opening it to have me hover only a foot away.

It takes a few moments, but then the door swings inward and Manon stands there, looking so elegant and posh, I can't imagine why she'd want me to enter at all.

Clearly, she does though. "Romi. Welcome. I'm so glad you're here. Come in." She backs up and holds the door open for me. "You can hang your coat there." She points to a small closet just inside. I know my coat is clean for the most part but still hesitate.

Manon seems to think it's because I'm shy or something, because she opens the, thankfully, empty closet and grabs a hanger. "Here. Let me take it for you."

Surreal. Manon Belmont, wealthier than anybody in East Quay, or even the East Coast for all I know, hangs my coat for me.

"This way. I thought we could make this a working lunch, if that's okay?"

"Sure. Thank you," I say. Another free meal. Two days in a row. Unheard of.

Manon guides me into what Aunt Clara would have called a winter garden, but I know others sometimes refer to it as a conservatory. Around us exotic plants grow in pots and raised beds. I recognize some of the specimens from pictures. Yucca palms seems to be popular in here, and they give the large space a rain-forest feel. In the center, a small, white cast-iron table with four chairs is set for two. Manon motions for me to sit down as a maid comes in with a cart full of food. To me it looks like way too much for two people, but who am I to complain?

"I thought a chicken pot pie with some salad and fruit might be a good choice." Manon places her napkin on her lap, and I do the same. "When it's chilly, like today, that's the perfect comfort food, I think. Thank you, Annette." She nods at the maid. "We'll be fine on our own now. Go on your break and tend to Wallace."

"Thank you, Manon. I will." Annette leaves, and I'm stunned that she and her employer are on a first-name basis.

"Wallace is Annette's husband. They live in the annex and have been with my family since I was in my twenties. Wallace needs some help, so I always make sure Annette has a two-hour lunch break."

"That's very generous," I say and accept the piece of pie Manon puts on my plate without showing how greedy for it I am.

"It's the least I can do. For someone as loyal to my family as they've been, they deserve nothing less." Manon nudges the salad bowl closer to me. "Dig in. Annette will be cross with us if we don't do our best to finish this lot off." She grins, which transforms her serious features into something so lovely and inviting, I nearly forget to eat.

After taking a few bites of the fantastic food, Manon rests her hands on the edge of the table, still holding her utensils. Her dark-chocolate hair lies in gentle waves around her shoulders, and she regards me with some curiosity. "Now. Tell me about yourself, dear."

I'm expecting the question, but that doesn't mean I know what to say. I'm not a good liar, but I'm pretty okay when it comes to dodging and avoiding questions—unless they're directed toward me with as much kindness and interest as Manon is expressing.

"Um. I…I don't know what to say really." I want to plead with Manon to just talk about that potential job with the choir and not ask anything of me that will destroy this possibility.

"Where were you born? Let's start with that."

That was a pretty safe question. "In Boston."

"And you just moved here from there?" Manon puts a piece of mushroom into her mouth and chews slowly while looking at me expectantly.

"No." I look down at the plate and wish I could just eat and not have to answer anything. Still, I know I'm here for an interview of sorts, so I try. "I came to East Quay when I was almost five. My mother died when I was four, and it took the authorities a while to find any living relative. I'm not sure how, exactly. My father died when I was even younger, and it was his only relative, an aunt by marriage, that I ended up with." Surely it must be okay to take a few more bites now? I eat more of the pie and then some salad.

"That's a rough start. Your father's aunt, does she live where we dropped you off?"

Shit. I drop my fork, which clatters as it lands on the plate. "She, um, did. Yes."

Manon doesn't seem to notice. "You may know, perhaps, that I run the Belmont Foundation. It reaches far into many communities here in Rhode Island. We used to have our main office in Providence, but we've moved it to East Quay since this is where I live when I'm not touring with Chicory Ariose." Manon takes another bite and sips her water before she continues. "I've come in contact with more than my fair share of kids and young people who need a helping hand. When I met you yesterday...I don't want to come off as presumptuous or as a know-it-all, but you struck me as a young woman in need of support."

I want to run out of there. I want to tell this wealthy woman with the kind eyes that I've been surviving for six years on my own without much help from anyone. I haven't yet resorted to begging in the street, unless you call busking begging. I suppose some might think of it that way, but I don't.

"This is hard. I realize that." Manon reaches across the table and briefly touches my right hand. "Charity, especially accepting it, is difficult."

She's right—and she's not. I don't mind charity—after all, I've stayed in shelters and eaten in soup kitchens provided by churches and private donors. For me, it's all about the spirit in which charity is given and what is expected in return. "Are you telling me that the choir-assistant position is a job that's construed to be charitable to someone like me?" I slowly raise my eyes from the food and lock them on Manon's. She doesn't waver.

"Not at all. We've discussed this subject on several occasions, ever since the choir leader, Carrie, started having to opt out occasionally. It's important that our girls in the choir have consistency and can depend on the choir on the days of practice. For some of them, it's their only constant except for school."

My interest grows despite my trepidations. The way Manon describes it, it doesn't sound like the wrong, demeaning kind of charity, where I would need to grovel. "Why me?" I don't mean to sound rude and fight to make my voice softer. "I mean, yes, you heard me sing, and I can carry a tune, but you have no idea who I am, if I'm trustworthy or even capable in any way."

Manon picks up a piece of cucumber with her fork but lets it hover between the plate and her mouth. "Good question. I didn't use to work on instinct, at least, not on instinct alone. Marrying Eryn and belonging to Chicory Ariose, I've had to learn to listen to what my gut tells me. Eryn and I both felt chills for all the right reasons when you sang that beautiful song, but when you joined us at the table, thanks to Tierney, who is a genuine force of nature, we both felt that you're the real thing. If you ask me to dissect our response to you, I can't. I suppose what it boils down to is a matter of taking a leap—and daring to trust. For you and me both."

"Not my strong point," I whisper, and the understanding reflected on Manon's face almost makes me cry. I've learned the hard way that if I dare to let the tears run, they won't stop. I don't cry, but I pick up the fork I dropped and spear a piece of lettuce.

"How long do you think you need to consider this offer?" Manon is done with her plate and leans back, placing her napkin next to it.

My neck smarts as I snap my head up to look at her. "I can't decline. I mean, I want to try." That doesn't come out right. Isn't a job interview all about showing self-confidence and knowing your worth and what you want? How can I show those traits when I really don't have any of them? What was it Aunt Clara used to say when I opposed any of her rules or orders? "Beggars can't be choosers." I don't realize that I've said it out loud before the words echo around me. I slap my hand over my mouth, and my tears are as close to overflowing as they've ever been without streaming down my cheeks.

"That's something someone's said to you enough times for it to fester, isn't it?" Manon's voice is soft, but thank God, she doesn't try to touch me or console me. "This is how this situation is going to play out." She reaches out to a shelf on the cart holding the food that I haven't noticed. Pulling out a folder and an expensive-looking pen, she motions for me to keep eating. "Full name, please?"

"Romi Shepherd."

"Age…twenty-two, was it?"

"Twenty-three in November."

"All right." Manon jots down the information. "Did you finish high school, Romi?"

My cheeks grow hot. "Not really. On paper, I mean."

Manon looks up, her eyebrows raised.

I push at a piece of cucumber, the last morsel on my plate. I'm full. An odd feeling, two days in a row. "I love libraries. I spent a lot of time there the last couple of years and tried to follow the last three years of the high school curriculum. I mean, I couldn't do any of the labs for chemistry and physics, but I know them in theory." I wonder if she thinks I'm bragging or, worse, lying. "It's true."

"Then we must make sure you get the chance to take your GED." She keeps writing. "I can tell you're a pro at shopping at thrift stores. Nothing wrong with that, but you're going to need a basic wardrobe to set a good example for the kids. Your coat is fine. I understand it's even in fashion."

I can't afford a new wardrobe. I won't even be able to get all new stuff if I get a part-time salary. Is she insane? I just stare at her, wondering how the hell I'll be able to tell her.

"And no, I haven't lost my marbles." Manon taps the back of her pen against the notes. "There's a store here in East Quay that my foundation has an account with. I'll call ahead and have Brittany help you out when you get there." Manon raised her free hand. "And before you object and think this is out of the ordinary, I promise you, it's not. The foundation has clothed all the girls in the choir, except for Stephanie, who nowadays comes from a well-to-do household. All the other girls are in foster care or come from low-income—or even non-income—homes.

"As the junior choir leader, you will have to get to know each girl and her background. You will also be required to let them know, to a degree, that your life has not been easy either. No details, other than what you're comfortable with, of course. When they see you, who are six to eight years older, and that you've survived and now lead and assist them—your example will make an impact." Manon grew serious, leaning forward. "This is the scope of the trust the foundation and I place in you.

If you can interact with the rest of the choir like you did with Steph and Lisa yesterday—you will work wonders."

My head is spinning. The way Manon speaks...she makes me think I can do it. That she sees something in me nobody else has and that she's certain I won't fail. Who am I to argue when everything inside me screams that this is my chance?

"I really want to." I see the faces of the girls in the choir— some with a gaunt look, some with newfound confidence, and some afraid of everything and anything. I straighten in my chair and I know I've turned a page, not only in my beloved notebook but in my life. If I can dare to reach out and help someone else, perhaps there's a chance for me, for a better life?

"There's one more thing, and it's non-negotiable." Manon leans forward and stares at me. "Before you start working, you'll have to submit to a drug test. As we're putting you in charge of young people, we have to make sure you don't have any serious substance-abuse problems. It's routine at the Belmont Foundation. A registered nurse will administer it, and the only ones who will see the results are her and me. HIPAA applies."

"I have no problem with that." This is one of the traps I've never fallen into, like so many of the people I came across when living on the streets of Manhattan. I was tempted sometimes, especially since some of the drugs took away hunger, but lack of money and fear of what it would turn me into made me keep my distance.

"Excellent. Just stop by the center and ask for the nurse. Should you need to address anything else regarding your health while you're there, it stays in your chart with her and has nothing to do with me."

As Manon follows me to the door after writing down phone numbers, the address to the clothes store, and next week's choir practice schedule, for me, she places her hand gently on my arm, stopping me.

"Come to think of it, what are you doing Friday evening?" she asks, tapping her chin.

"Um. Nothing?"

"We're invited to a dinner party, Eryn and I, and I know Stephanie will be there as well. Why don't you come as our guest? I know our hostesses won't mind, as they tell us constantly to bring friends. It's casual attire, so anything you pick out at the store will do."

I'm sure I've misunderstood. "A dinner party?"

"Yes."

"But I've never been to one." Panic lurks behind my words, and I wonder if Manon picks up on it.

"It's the same as what we just did, but with a few more people. Everyone there will be friendly, and you needn't worry. You already know half the gang from yesterday." Manon smiles broadly. "Please say you'll come?"

My head spins, but I can't deny this woman anything. She feels, well, not maternal, exactly, but so very caring and honest. If she didn't truly want me to come with them, then she didn't have to mention a dinner party I knew nothing about, did she?

"Thank you. Should I come here first…or…?" I step outside after retrieving my jacket.

"Yes, that's a good idea. Their house is among the dunes and not easy to spot unless you know where to go. If you get here at six thirty, that'll give us plenty of time."

I thank Manon again and then walk down the flagstone garden path. When I turn to look at the house again, I see her still standing there, leaning against the doorframe, one leg crossed over the other. She waves at me and then walks back in, closing the door behind her.

As I make my way toward the center of East Quay, my thoughts whirl constantly in my head. One sentence keeps popping up to the surface, no matter how I try to whack-a-mole it.

How the hell did this happen?

CHAPTER EIGHT

Gail

I disconnect the cell phone after hanging up with Neill. He and Laurence aren't going to be able to join me at Vivian's tonight, which makes me feel relieved and uneasy at the same time. Getting stuck in traffic in Manhattan isn't new, but when you drive like Neill, like a snail on Valium, it takes you even longer. They'll get here tonight, but two hours later than they thought. I told him I'd leave the key for them under a big stone on the northeast corner of the house, as I don't expect to be home when they arrive.

After texting Vivian to let her and Mike know I won't be bringing the guys, I toss the phone onto the bed and stare at the so-called choices before me. I refuse to second-guess myself. I hate any type of indecision, hesitation, or ambiguity—especially within myself. Standing in front of the closet, I see my options are limited, which helps with any such potential character flaws. It's a good thing Vivian's dinner party is casual, since I didn't bother to bring any of my more elegant clothes. But, considering my orthosis and sling, I can't wear just anything.

Eventually I pick a white, flowy shirt with arms wide enough to accommodate the orthosis. It's buttoned in the front, and I can manage that even if it takes ten times as long as it used to. Black slacks are always appropriate, no matter how casual the hosts say the party is. I pull on my black ankle boots and then brush through my hair. Since the accident, I haven't been able to wear it in any elaborate hairdos other than loose, pulled back in a twist with a special clasp, or with a headband. I choose a broad, black, glossy headband that will keep my hair out of my face. I've learned the hard way that, with one hand, it's quite the chore to keep pushing at my hair while trying to manage a fork. Cutting meat is still damn near impossible. The occupational therapist offered me a large number of tools to help with that and other challenges, but I blew her off. I never used to regret being harsh like that, but truth be told, I've thought of that kind woman several times and wished I'd harnessed myself better.

I pull on the faux-fur jacket, then place some painkillers in my clutch, along with a credit card and my driver's license. A quick check in the hallway mirror reassures me the discreet makeup I applied after my shower is intact.

The drive to Vivian and Mike's place is uneventful until I arrive. I park where another one of Vivian's texts suggested and look for the path between the dunes. Cursing under my breath, I can't find it. It's supposed to be a wooden walkway with hand railings. Feeling ridiculous, I step onto the sand, hoping to see well enough in the dark to find it. The text should have suggested a flashlight.

"Hello there. Let me guess. You're on your way to see Mike and Vivian," an amused voice behind me states.

I turn around. A willowy young woman with curly, auburn hair stands a few steps away from me, beside another woman, this one blond, and a teenage girl. Next to the other woman, a black dog in a harness is pressed up against her leg.

"Yes, I am." I extend my left hand. "I'm Gail."

"Tierney. This is my wife, Giselle, and our daughter, Stephanie."

"Nice to meet you. I hope you know the way, because I'm

bound to get lost among the dunes if I try this on my own." I have
to return Tierney's contagious smile.

"Don't feel bad," Stephanie says. "You wouldn't be the first
one Vivian has sent Perry and Mason out to locate."

"Perry and Mason?" I crinkle my nose while envisioning
two overly muscular bodyguards.

"Her Great Danes. Those boys know every grain of sand on
this beach."

Danish bodyguards? Then I feel silly. "Ah. Dogs. I see." I
follow as the trio begins to round one of the larger dunes. I see a
light now and realize there is indeed a walkway, lit by small LED
lanterns. Thankfully, the house is closer than I thought. When it
comes into view, its well-lit windows and patio lanterns make the
house on stilts resemble a jewel glowing in the dark.

"Here we are!" Stephanie takes the six steps in two strides
and rings the doorbell.

Apparently, Mike has been standing just inside the door
since she opens it so quickly, Stephanie takes a hasty step back.
"Whoa!"

"Sorry, Steph." Mike grins broadly. She seems comfortable
enough in her own skin, yet I have a feeling this perhaps wasn't
always the case. I see a resemblance in the way she moves to
how Romi carries herself, with smooth, cautious movements,
as if trying to avoid predatory individuals. Not sure where these
thoughts come from, I shake them off. No use indulging in
groundless speculations.

"Gail. You made it." Vivian meets me as I step over the
threshold. "Tierney, Giselle…and my darling Stephanie. Have
you all introduced yourselves?"

I'm impressed that she's already picked up on which guests
have arrived. "We have. Thank you. And I'm glad you didn't
have to send your dogs out after me." I glance at Stephanie, who
grins.

"What? Oh. You found the walkway hard to locate? It's

deliberate, to keep people and, I must admit, ardent fans away as much as possible. I should've asked Mike to give you more visual cues." Vivian holds out her hand for my jacket and hangs it in a small alcove. "Why don't you and I walk straight through the house and into the living room. Mike has champagne on ice." She takes my good arm, and we stroll through the beach house. Like the restaurant, it's decorated in the New England style, but much more personal and with stunning art pieces—figurines, statues, and paintings.

"I love your house," I say. "It's very beautiful—and I can tell you're collectors."

"Thank you. I rented it at first from some good friends but managed to convince them to sell after I knew I wanted to make East Quay my base—and live my life with Mike." Vivian squeezes my arm gently "I collected most of the paintings before I lost my vision. Nowadays, Mike purchases them and does a great job describing them to me. I love the statues, as I can see them through touch. I never thought I'd be inclined to go all tactile like this. I used to be the queen of air kisses. As little touching as possible—always afraid of catching a virus."

"I've turned those air kisses into an art form as well. Until lately." I haven't kissed anyone, or the air around them, for that matter, for a long time. I was never concerned about catching some virus, but I always needed a lot of personal space. Neill used to joke that was the reason I became a soloist. No rubbing elbows next to other musicians. He wasn't all that wrong.

I stop on the threshold to the living room. It's clearly a new extension to the beach house, placed at a ninety-degree angle to the rest of the house. At the far end, the one closest to the water, sits a Steinway grand piano, which is not a surprise. The fact that it's joined by a multitude of instruments on the walls, including two violins, makes my heart beat so hard, I'm sure Vivian must be able to pick up the sound.

I haven't seen a violin up close since I went in for my second surgery, which I was certain would restore the use of my right arm. When it failed, I had my housekeeper clear out the music room before I was discharged from the hospital. I thought it was the right thing to do as I couldn't imagine looking at my instruments. As it turned out, the empty walls hurt me even more since they reflected perfectly how I felt inside. Empty. Cold. Barren. Without purpose.

Now I stare at the violins, and the fingers of my left hand move of their own volition, as if they want to seek out the strings and play. One of Biber's *Mystery Sonatas*, perhaps. That was one of the pieces I was rehearsing for the Carnegie Hall concert that was only two weeks away when I had my accident.

"What's the matter, dear?" Vivian lets go of my arm and instead places a hand on the small of my back. "You're trembling."

"Nothing." I swallow hard. "Just dizzy there for a moment. Guess I'm hungry." I lie like my life hangs in the balance. In fact, I'm nauseous and can't figure out how I'll be able to eat at all.

Vivian doesn't answer right away, but then her warm smile reappears. "Good thing Mike's favorite chef at the restaurant has cooked up a virtual storm."

"Yes. Good thing," I say weakly, fighting to get a grip on my damn nerves.

I hear new voices and more guests arrive. I take a glass of a non-alcoholic beverage and turn to politely greet them when they join us.

"Ah, it's Manon and Eryn." Vivian sips her champagne. "And they're bringing a mystery guest. We love that. Another thing that has changed for me. I used to be quite the hermit in between performances. By the way, sorry that your friends were delayed. I hope we get to meet them another time." She smooths down her gently teased hair and walks toward the hallway. As she crosses the floor, she seems entirely aware of each obstacle that might have otherwise tripped her.

When I'm alone, I greedily draw new oxygen into my lungs, which helps me regain a sense of calm. *They're just instruments. They're not even mine. Get a fucking grip.*

Steps approach, and a lithe, dark-haired woman walks in next to Vivian, who introduces us. "Gail, this is my friend and band member, Manon Belmont."

I greet Manon, whom I've read about in the local newspaper online, and I know she and her foundation are revered for their commitment to those in need of help.

"Gail Owen? The violinist?" Manon tilts her head, and then her even gaze falls to my sling. "Oh, my. That was clumsy of me. I'm sorry."

"Don't mention it," I say, calm now. "It is what it is."

"Of course," Manon says and changes the subject. "Seems that most of us here tonight are musically inclined one way or another. And speaking of that, let me introduce you both to our latest friend—and believe me—she's a true find. Romi? Join me, please."

Romi? Surely…I gape for a few moments before I realize what I'm doing and snap my mouth closed.

Romi steps into the living room beside a taller woman with red hair kept in a long braid. Looking shy, but not ill at ease, she glances around the room—and then she sees me. Growing several shades paler, she flinches and appears ready to bolt, but then she stays right there, as if glued to the carpet.

"Hello, Romi," I say coolly. "What a surprise."

"You know each other?" Mike says as she joins us. "What a coincidence."

Manon hands the redhead a glass of champagne. "My wife Eryn and I only got to know Romi a little bit the other day at open-mic night. She has a marvelous voice."

I raise a deliberate eyebrow at Romi. "She does?"

"Absolutely," Manon says and wraps an arm around Eryn's waist. "This is Eryn. She used to run the local newspaper. Nowadays she's the liaison between us and our agent and management team, when she's not strumming that guitar of hers. Eryn, this is Gail."

"Wow. Thank you for that amazing introduction," Eryn

says, but laughs and tosses her long braid back over her shoulder. "Hello, Gail. Nice to meet you." She merely waves her fingers at me. "Strumming my guitar, huh?"

"Please. Without you we'd be dead in the water, not knowing where to go or what to do. And you're an electric-guitar virtuoso." Vivian stepped closer to Eryn. "Now, I want to know how Gail and—Romi, was it?—know each other." She holds her hand out in Romi's direction, whose complexion changes from pale to pink. "Welcome to our beach house."

"Thank you for having me. I mean, for allowing me to tag along." Romi takes Vivian's hand in a lightning-fast shake.

I clear my voice, confused at how jittery I feel. I don't even acknowledge the concept of jitters, normally. "We're neighbors. Romi has been kind enough to help me with some heavy lifting." Self-conscious now, I know full well my words don't come out right.

"Heavy lifting?" Manon blinks, no doubt taking Romi's slight stature into consideration.

"I'm stronger than I look, Manon," Romi says, her voice low, but she raises her chin.

"I'll say." I know I've made Romi beyond uncomfortable, and for some reason, this makes my stomach ache. "And very helpful."

Romi regards me in silence for a moment. And then she does something that changes the tense ambiance in the room.

She smiles.

Chapter Nine

Romi

Gail is here. We're inexplicably at the same dinner party—and considering it's my first dinner party ever, it's beyond coincidental. The freaking universe is conspiring against me to rub my nose in the fact that I'm taking advantage of this woman, compromising her privacy, and generally being a total lowlife.

As everyone seems so dead set on finding out how I could possibly be acquainted with this amazing woman, who is on a completely different tier than I am, I see something I never expected. Gail looks nervous. What the—? I let my gaze travel between the women standing in a semicircle in the large living room, and then I spot something at the far wall. Instruments. And not just the grand piano, which is the first thing you see as it dominates the room. Violins. That has to suck for Gail. A few days ago, she seemed skinless when she talked about how her injury had changed everything. I haven't seen any sheets of music or any instruments at the farmhouse. And here she stands, among quite the crowd of musicians, plus me, surrounded by reminders of what she's lost.

"Heavy lifting?" Manon says incredulously, and I realize that Gail has told the others that I've helped her. Did she tell them she paid me too? I cringe. I wish I'd listened better.

"I'm stronger than I look, Manon." I square my shoulders.

"I'll say." Gail's voice is gentler than I've ever heard it. "And very helpful."

Wow. Now I can't resist a broad smile from forming on my face. Something about how Gail sounds, as if she wants me to know she has my back, or something, makes me giddy. An unusual sensation, to say the last.

"Helpful." Vivian raises her glass to us. "That's how I met Mike. She was helpful and sweet, and I, despite my diva habits, fell in love."

Gail blushes, and I nearly slap my hand over my gaping mouth. Does Vivian know how that sounds? What she seems to imply? I want to groan and hide, but I pretend like I never noticed the suggestive words. Sneaking another glimpse of Gail, I see her place the glass of champagne on a sideboard and excuse herself. The others are in the midst of reminiscing how they all met, which is confusing as hell when you weren't present when it all occurred.

"They're going to be at it for a while. Not the first time they go all 'remember when.'" Stephanie joins me and motions toward a smaller room next to the living room. "Want to meet the boys?"

"The boys?" I blink and wonder if Vivian and Mike have kids, before I remember the dogs. "You sure that's okay? How are they with strangers?" I've been bitten three damn times by dogs in New York, in the subway. One poodle, one dachshund, and one dog of indistinguishable origin have sunk their sharp teeth into me, twice in my calves and once between my thumb and index fingers. I was glad I never came down with either rabies or tetanus, since there was no way I could pay for a vaccine or treatment. The dog owners sure weren't going to cough up the money for someone like me.

"They're two goofballs, and they're getting old too. Big dogs like Great Danes don't have a super-long life expectancy. I know Vivian stresses about it. They're brothers." Stephanie walks into the smaller room, and there, two majestic dogs have taken over a white leather couch. Someone has covered most of it with some blankets, but the dogs managed to bunch them up before they lay down.

"Hi, guys." Stephanie kneels before the one to the left and frames his large face with her hands. "You're such a handsome boy, Perry." She gazes at me over her shoulder. "Why don't you pat Mason before he feels left out?"

I swallow but don't want to come across as a coward. I used to really like dogs, before I came to New York. I mimic Stephanie and crouch before the enormous dog. "Hi, Mason. I'm Romi."

Mason tilts his head, and his soft ears change positions. I hold out my hand under his chin, so he can sniff it. Aunt Clara taught me this move and said it worked with most animals. Never approach from above in a threatening manner, always from underneath.

Mason sniffs me, and then I get a discreet lick. I start to relax and prepare to pat him, when I feel a distinct pressure against my back. I'm entirely unprepared and fall sideways with a loud yelp. I stare at the black leather armchair next to the couch that seems to have come alive. Giselle's black retriever sits there, her tongue lolling, and she's waving her paw at me.

"Charley!" Stephanie sounds strict as she points at the smiling dog. "Are you trying to give Romi a heart attack?"

Several steps approach, and Mike, Giselle, and Tierney crowd the doorway. And of course, Gail has returned from wherever she went. Super.

"What happened?" Mike hurries over and extends a hand. "Are you all right, Romi?"

I feel so ridiculous now, I could howl. "I'm fine."

"She didn't scratch you, did she?" Stephanie comes over, still on her knees. "Charley got jealous and tried to pat Romi on the back for attention. She still has some manners challenges."

"No scratches," I say, and accept Mike's hand, not only to be polite toward her gesture, but because my hip smarts again. "I didn't see her in the black chair, that's all." I want to sink through the floor.

"Thank God you didn't hurt yourself on the coffee table." Mike puts an arm around my shoulders and squeezes briefly. "What a terrible impression we're making on you."

"Not at all. I'm just not used to dogs nowadays." I shrug, and for some reason I find myself looking for Gail. She notices and takes a few steps toward me.

"Stronger than you look, right?" she says, the corners of her mouth curling slightly.

"Exactly," I say, and now I can smile for real.

"I think we need food after all this excitement. The dogs are not allowed in the dining room." Vivian waves at us as she raises that amazing voice to get our attention.

The dining room is all in white and light blue, except the hardwood floor that is made of dark oak. No curtains hinder the view of the ocean, where large waves crash onto the beach. The house is raised on stilts, like most beach houses, and I hope Vivian and Mike know how lucky they are to live here.

I'm not surprised when I end up sitting across from Gail. I have Stephanie to one side, which I think she made sure of by squeezing by Tierney, who barely managed to sit down. To my right, I have Manon, which feels reassuring. She's the one who knows a little more about me. It's thanks to her that I now have a basic wardrobe, a cell phone, and a part-time job when my drug test passes muster, which I know it will.

I look furtively at Gail, who is arranging her utensils with her left hand. Will she need help? No. She would never ask for help like that—nor would she even want it. I pray we're not having some humongous steaks, or anything that will render her unwanted attention.

The starter dish is shrimp cocktail, something I've seen but never eaten. I check the others out, to see how they approach this dish. Mike, Tierney, and Stephanie simply pick up the shrimp by the tail using their hands, while the others use their smaller forks.

Screw it. I won't fiddle with a miniature fork. I take the shrimp, dip it in the red sauce like I see the others do, and take a bite. My taste buds go into orbit. The different flavors, the textures, all create something in my mouth that I've never experienced. I blink at threatening tears and feel so silly that I'm ready to bolt to the bathroom to hide my reaction.

"You okay?" Stephanie whispers, leaning in.

"Mmm-hmm." I chew and swallow. "Yes."

"I remember the first time I had this. I thought I'd died and gone to heaven." Stephanie speaks quietly enough to not draw attention, or so I think until I look across the table and my eyes meet Gail's. Crap.

"Never had it before either," I murmur to Stephanie. "More used to cheeseburgers. That sort of thing."

"I hear you. You should have seen me taste my first real eggs when I came to stay with Tierney and Giselle. I'd only had that powdered stuff where I stayed before." Something dark ghosts across Stephanie's face. "I live such a different life now, I have to pinch myself every single day."

"I'm happy you ended up in a good place." I'm envious, to be honest, but not begrudging.

"It will happen for you too." Stephanie looks at me, her young face knowing in a way that makes me nervous as hell. "And don't worry. I'm not a blabbermouth. Just so you know." She nudges me with her knee under the table. "We're cool."

I relax. Stephanie is very cool, actually. My eyes meet Gail's again, and I think I see a puzzled expression on her face, which is odd since she usually assumes an indifferent, or sometimes disdainful, look.

The main course is also from the ocean—salmon and a multitude of vegetables, all presented in bite-size pieces. I wonder if Vivian and Mike have thought of Gail being only able to use one hand to eat when they came up with the menu. If so, these are amazing friends to have. Either way, now Gail doesn't have to stand out as the only one needing assistance. I think the music-room shock was enough for her. After she left the room, I bet she bolted for the bathroom like I wanted to do just moments ago.

I mainly listen to the conversation around the table as I force myself to eat at the same pace as the others, trying to not come across as if I expect someone to yank the plate away from me before I'm done. Manon brings me into the conversation every now and then, and I begin to relax further—until she announces that I'm going to work as a junior choir leader at the Belmont Foundation.

Gail's eyebrows shoot up, and I want to groan out loud but don't.

"That's fantastic!" Vivian claps her hands together. "I hear you have a lovely voice."

"She does, but it's more than that. I have a knack for finding people who can bring more than that to a group of young people who need to feel they belong." Manon smiles brightly and squeezes my hand on the table. "I suppose it comes from working with support staff and social workers for many years. And when Eryn immediately seconded my opinion, I knew I was definitely onto something."

"I know Romi will be great. I mean, Carrie is wonderful, but it'll be wonderful to have someone closer in age as well. Especially when it comes to helping us choose songs." Stephanie grins.

"Do you hope for a chance in show business yourself, Romi?" Giselle asks, and though her voice is kind, I can tell she's cautious.

"No, not at all. That's not what I want." And it's the truth. I used my voice in the New York subway because it was one of my chances to make money, but that's where it stopped being my dream. I enjoy singing, but doing it that way, among people ranging from indifferent or scornful to mildly appreciative, cured my former dreams about being in the limelight.

"Then what do you see yourself doing down the line?" Giselle's smile warms her features.

"I'm still figuring things out, but I know I'm not meant for show business." I tuck my hands between my knees.

"Please stop giving Romi the third degree," Vivian says as if sensing my growing discomfort. "Let's just be glad Manon found the right person for the choir."

"You're right. Enough with the questions." Manon turns to Giselle, who sits across from her, and soon they're discussing some joint venture.

I look at the dessert that the guy waiting on us places before me. Ice cream with an amazing chocolate sauce dripping down on top of pieces of some citrus fruit I don't recognize. I use the only utensil that's left, a small spoon, and dig in.

"Good, huh?" Gail says, and I see her eyes sparkle as she takes a spoonful. "No, not good. Divine."

I decide I like the dessert best of all tonight. I've never been able to indulge any type of sweet tooth very much since I left East Quay. When I lived with Aunt Clara, she made great desserts, mainly fruit pies, and we sometimes had ice cream. I occasionally used some of the money I earned for mowing lawns and babysitting for some candy, but not very often, as I was saving up to leave as soon as I could. After going to New York, I ran out of money so fast, I certainly never again had any left to spend on candy. It would have been easy, in a way, since some cheap candy would have staved off my hunger temporarily, but like drugs, I saw what that did to people as well. Sugar crashes and bad teeth can kill you almost as fast.

"Love it," I say to Gail now. "So good."

Once we've all stuffed ourselves completely full, we go back to the living room. I notice Gail chooses an armchair that sits with its back toward the instruments. So, maybe I was right.

Then Gail's phone rings and she excuses herself. Walking back into the dining room, she talks quietly, but her voice grows concerned. As she returns, she looks at Vivian and Mike. "I apologize that I have to cut this short. I'm having a really good time, but I need to get back to the house. My friends from out of town can't locate the key, and I can't keep them waiting in their car."

"Oh, dear," Vivian says, a worried frown on her face. "I don't suppose they'll want to drive over to us after such a long trip already, even if they'd be most welcome?"

"If I know Neill, he'd be mortified not arriving to meet all of you without looking his absolute best." Gail rounds the table and places her good hand on Vivian's shoulder. "Thank you for the lovely dinner. I'm sorry for cutting it short. We'll see each other again soon, I hope." She sounds sincere, but something in her voice sounds like apprehension, or at least cautiousness.

"Absolutely, Gail." Vivian gets up and wraps an arm around her, clearly mindful of her injured arm. "And I think we need to meet tomorrow, at the café, for a quick cup, if nothing else. I have a feeling your friends are as interesting as you."

Gail chuckles, and the sound permeates something well hidden inside me, making me shiver. "All right, Vivian. Who am I to argue with that? I know Neill and Laurence were heartbroken to miss you all." Gail nods amicably to the rest of us sitting around the table. Her eyes stop for a second when she looks at me. "I don't suppose you want to cut the dinner party short in order to get a lift home, Romi?" she asks casually.

I'm torn. As enjoyable as some of this is, it's damn intimidating, and I've struggled with feeling out of my depth on and off since I stepped over the threshold. Truthfully, I'm exhausted.

"We'll drive Romi home, as she came with us," Manon says. "Unless you'd rather hitch a ride with Gail?" she asks, turning to me.

Oh, great. If I say yes, I may offend my hosts, and if I say no, I may offend—nah, who am I kidding? Gail won't care one way or the other if I ride home with her or not. I open my mouth, fully intending to say that I'll stay, when I see her cradling her arm. She's in pain. Yes, she drives an automatic, but going home in the dark and having to back out of that narrow parking lot behind the dunes with one arm…she might just need my company. Of course, I'm useless in a car since I don't drive, but still. A small, inner voice chides me that I'm simply making up a reason for a chance to be alone with this woman who constantly invades my mind, but I silence it by standing up.

"I'd be grateful if I can ride home with you," I say, my voice firm. Not forgetting the solid manners my aunt instilled in me, I walk over to Vivian and Mike and thank them for their hospitality. Vivian hugs me, this time squeezing much harder than she did with Gail.

Mike sees us out after I've said good-bye to the others and helps Gail pull her coat securely around her orthosis. The only sign of how much it must hurt is the small frown between Gail's eyebrows. I pray Mike knows better than to try to button the coat for Gail, and I'm not disappointed.

"You must come to the café tomorrow too," Mike says to me and then bends to kiss my cheek, which is so unexpected that I nearly stumble. Uncertain how to reciprocate, or even if I should, I merely nod and shove my hands into my back pockets. "I'll try. Thank you."

"Cool. See you then." Mike opens the door for us and remains there until Gail and I have walked down the steps to the wooden path. Then she waves and closes it.

Chapter Ten

Romi

I walk next to Gail, and I wouldn't even dream of offering her my arm, unless she asked for support. Somehow, I imagine she has had enough of reminders tonight about her injured arm. Well, not the arm per se, but what it has cost her. She doesn't need to have me fawn over her.

"Thanks for offering to drive me home," I say. "I'm really grateful they accepted me as an extra guest, but I'm not used to that type of social setting and was starting to feel a bit, well, kind of jittery." It's not untrue, and I don't want Gail to realize it was her vulnerability, or what I perceived as such, that tipped the scale for my leaving early.

"No problem. After all, we're neighbors."

These simple words bring the guilt of lying to her, of trespassing like a damn stalker, forward and crashing down on me. "Yes. We are."

Gail turns her head quickly to look at me. Perhaps something in my voice gave me away, but I'm not sure. "You all right?"

"I'm fine."

"You've fallen twice in a few days." Gail sounds suspicious, and I can't have her think I'm injured.

"I promise. I'm totally okay." I try to infuse perkiness in my voice, which is entirely alien to me. I don't do perky any more than Gail does.

"Hmm. I have to take your word for it. By the way, I like your new outfit."

Now I'm starting to think that it's Gail who has banged her head or something. "What? Um. Thank you?" I feel a need to explain, as she's only seen me in thrift-store stuff before. "I got an advance as I need to look a little more professional on Monday." It's almost true. Salaries aren't always paid in cash. I try for a smile but don't think it can look very natural.

"And you do look professional. The style suits you." Gail stops by her car and presses the fob in her hand.

I get into the passenger seat and use my peripheral vision to search for signs of Gail's pain level. As it turns out, I don't have to be this cautious. Gail groans as she slumps back into her seat.

"Fuck." She closes her eyes hard.

I don't know what to say, but I know not to express any pity. I go for matter-of-fact. "Want help buckling up?"

Gail breathes deeply twice before answering. "Yes." Her voice is strangled, and I ache for her.

Shifting in my seat, I'm glad I'm the skinny type as I need to lean past her to reach the belt. I don't want to accidentally brush against her arm. I tug gently at the belt and pull it across her, mindful not to apply pressure anywhere. "Can you raise your arm just a little, so I can fasten it?"

Holding her arm away from her body, Gail is trembling now. "Damn it. I don't suppose you drive, do you?"

"Sorry. No license."

"Well, I'm going to need you to put the car in reverse when I start." Gail looks at me, and her eyes glisten in the muted light from the two street lights.

"Sure."

Gail presses the button next to the wheel and nods at me. I pull at the stick, remembering to push the button that makes it possible to move it, sliding it into the R slot.

"Now into drive mode," Gail says after backing up. She maneuvers the wheel with practiced ease, but the pain level makes her bite her lips.

"Can't you get one of those knobs that truck drivers have?" I know I could be overstepping, but her pain chisels away at the walls I erected around my heart a long time ago. If she gets mad at me, so be it.

"I've never thought about that." Gail sends me a quick glance. "Could come in handy, I suppose."

Wow. Almost praise, coming from Gail. "Just an idea." I decide to shut up and not push my luck.

Gail seems to be content not talking, much like when we drove to the bank the other day. I don't find the silence awkward, which is both surprising—and not. I rarely do well when I have to keep up a conversation, but prolonged silence can still weird me out. Now, I sit next to this woman whom I'm becoming so protective of, and... My mind stalls. And what? I look over at Gail, who now sits more relaxed as we've reached the main road, and traffic is light. Her profile is strong with a determined chin, high cheekbones, and a slightly bent nose. She squints some, but I don't think it's from being nearsighted, but rather from the pain. The blond hair, kept back from her stunning face by a wide headband, tumbles around her shoulders, and my fingers itch to touch it, run through it to assess if it's as silky as it looks.

"You're staring." Gail doesn't look at me, but I can see her eyebrows rise.

Shit. "Um. Sorry?" What the hell's wrong with me? This is so not me. I keep my distance, I remain as safe as I can, I keep my guard up as much as it humanly possible...And now...now I can't take my eyes off Gail, and all I think of instead of self-preservation is to protect her.

"No need to apologize. I'm simply curious as to why." Gail manages to sound entirely indifferent, of course.

"You're beautiful." Oh, God. What the hell was in those damn shrimps? Something that made me lose my mind, clearly. I snap my jaws closed so fast, I fear my molars might shatter. I still can't take my eyes off her.

Gail grips the wheel harder, but that's the only way I can tell she heard me. At least she doesn't offer another impassive comment. All I have to do is keep my mouth tightly shut and I won't dig my hole any deeper. Hopefully.

"Yet again," Gail murmurs.

"Excuse me?" I ignore my intention to be quiet in two seconds flat.

"You managed to surprise me yet again. It rarely happens." Gail snorts, but it's not a particularly happy sound.

"Is that a good or a bad thing? I mean, surprising you?" Now I turn slightly in my seat to be able to look at her without getting a kink in my neck.

"The jury's still out on that one." Gail smiles now, which I suppose is an improvement.

"It's not something I plan."

This makes her chuckle for the second time during the evening. Like before, it gives me shivers, but this time even more so since something I said caused it. Never in my life have I responded this way to someone else. I don't want to stop looking at her, ever, and I have no idea what it is that makes me shiver. It's mostly a pleasurable feeling, but it also scares the crap out of me.

"Ah, we're almost home. Where should I drop you off?" Gail seems relieved, and who can blame her.

"Your driveway's fine. I don't have far to go," I say, turning forward again. The other conversation is obviously over, most likely for good.

"You sure?"

"Yes." I hope she won't insist on suddenly wanting to drop me off at "my house."

"All right." Gail turns off the main road. "And there are Neill and Laurence."

"Just let me get out here, and you can go greet your friends." My words tumble out of my mouth so fast, I nearly stutter.

"Don't be ridiculous—"

"Please. I'd like to just go home from here." I realize I sound like I'm begging, and who the hell am I kidding? I'm pleading so I don't have to be introduced to these friends of hers. I've had my fill of new acquaintances today and can't take another "this is Romi, she helps me with heavy lifting" remark. Not after how I've been emotionally tumble-dried this evening.

"All right, all right." Gail stops the car.

I reach for the handle, about to bolt.

"Hold it." Gail suddenly sounds strained. "Please. Do me a favor and unbuckle my seat belt? I'd rather not…not demonstrate the pain level tonight to the guys."

"Oh. Sure." I press the button to release her belt, mindful to keep it from touching her. I follow it over into its slot next to the door and start to ease back when she places her good hand on my shoulder, stopping me. "Gail?"

"Thank you," she whispers. Our faces are so close, I can feel her breathing against my face. Her scent, something dark but not heavy, reminds me of black currants, engulfs me.

"You're welcome," I say just as quietly, which seems to amuse her because I get chuckle number three for the evening.

I close my eyes for a few moments, even though there's no risk she'll read something in them in the dark. "Good night," I say and pull back slowly. "Thank you for the ride."

"Good night."

I step out of the car and walk in my usual fake direction. Then I double back when I see Gail has exited the car and is standing in the circle of the porch light with two men. I know it'll blind them for what goes on in the darkness around them.

As I make my way into the basement and then the secret room, I vow to myself that come Monday, I won't return here. I cannot do this to Gail any longer. It's not right.

I have no clue where I'll sleep from Monday onward, but the situation isn't new to me, after all. At least, that's what I tell myself. The situation isn't new—but I've changed.

I curl up on the bed, praying that I won't hear any confessions in the spy corner tonight. Surely the guys will be hungry or something, and they'll be in the dining room or the kitchen?

I can't handle any more right now.

CHAPTER ELEVEN

Gail

"You're sure you're not pulling my leg?" Neill says as he pulls out of my driveway. He's offered to drive, which I gladly accepted since my arm is even worse today. If this keeps up, I'll have to see a local physiotherapist this coming week, whether I want to or not.

"I'm not pulling anything, yet. But I may pull off your nearest protruding body part if you don't stop nagging me," I reply, which makes Laurence laugh where he sits in the back seat.

"I swear this is nothing compared to last night. Neill kept going on and on about Chicory Ariose in general and Vivian Harding in particular, and how he nearly *died* of disappointment when we hit such traffic and he missed her dinner party." Laurence sighs. "You'd think she was the queen."

"She is!" Neill turns his bald head over his shoulder and glares at his fiancé. "Vivian Harding is the most amazing mezzo-soprano that ever lived. The music she creates with Chicory Ariose has placed her in her very own category. Have you really heard of any other opera singers who can improvise and do what she does with them? I think not!"

Neill huffs and I smile, but also tune out their familiar type of banter. I spent most of last night talking about anything and everything, except what was on my mind, and now my brain insists I think of her. Of Romi.

What the hell happened last night in the car? She was, of course, being sweet and helpful, but that wasn't it. She stopped moving and my eyes got stuck in hers. I mean, that never happens to me. I've never been one for sappy, romantic stuff. No time for that. I've had my share of lovers, men and women, whenever my schedule has permitted it, but mainly for sex…and to have someone escort me to events. The music world can be as judgmental as any other, and though I've never minded my own company, my pride prevented me from arriving somewhere important alone.

No. Not once have I lost my breath and gotten lost in someone's eyes—and most certainly, if someone had tried such a thing with me back then, I'd have scoffed and made sure they didn't "get stuck" again.

I retrace what happened last night. I had been surprised at how Romi looked better put together and not as if her clothes were going to fall off her body because of wear and tear. The fact that she arrived with Manon Belmont, who may or may not be responsible for Romi's wardrobe improvement, was beyond unexpected. Learning that Romi can sing had given me pause, but her objecting to wanting to pursue music as a profession sounded genuine, though that might be an act, for all I know. She also startled me when I realized she fell over in the company of the huge dogs. The girl is thin enough for a strong wind to blow her away to damn Kansas, after all.

I'm not sure if I was imagining it, but I had the feeling she was deliberately pacing herself while eating. Do the people she lives with not provide her with food *or* clothes? Yes, she's an adult, yet…It doesn't make sense, and it's certainly not right.

The guys are still going on about the pros and cons of classical training when singing, and I lean my head back and cradle my arm. I never did catch what kind of song Romi performed when she caught Manon's and Eryn's attention. Apparently, Giselle and Tierney were present, and the young girl as well, Stephanie, during open-mic night.

Last night, when I offered Romi a lift, I didn't pay attention to any particular undertone. I simply asked as I tried to do the small-town thing and be neighborly. I mean, how would it have looked if I drove home and ignored a young woman who lived so close to me? This last thought derails my mind again. She lives so close to me, but where? She never volunteers any such information, and something tells me she's ashamed of humble beginnings. Is it my wealth or status—or former status as it were—that makes her clam up? I know I intimidate some people quite easily, but with her, I'm not sure that's why she's tight-lipped about her actual address. I'm fairly sure she lives northeast of me, but I've never seen any lights that way, so it must be a bit farther than she lets on.

"Is that perhaps the enigmatic Romi you don't want me to ask too much about?" Neill asks and startles me out of my train of thought.

I straighten my back and look out the windscreen. It is indeed Romi. We're about five minutes from East Quay, and here she is walking along the side of the road.

"It is." I open my mouth to ask Neill to pull up, but he beats me to it.

I roll down the window, suddenly mindful of not startling Romi by showing up in a strange car. "Hello." I lose what polite greeting I meant to add after that one word as she turns to look at me. Her eyes are huge, and the intensity of her gaze makes my stomach tense.

"Hi, Gail." Romi takes a step back, away from the car.

"We're heading to have lunch at the Sea Stone Café. Jump in." I point toward the back seat.

"Ah. Um. No, thank you, that's not necessary. I've called Mike and Vivian and canceled. I need to prepare for tomorrow." Romi kicks at the dirt at her feet.

"Oh, no," Neill says and leans across me to look at Romi,

inadvertently nudging my bad arm. I hiss and pull away from him. "Fuck. Sorry, Gail. I'm an idiot. I'm just so disappointed that I won't get to meet your Romi."

I want to smack him for making the pain soar in my arm, but mainly for calling Romi "mine." Now I see how Romi hesitates, and before I quite realize my intention, I've unbuckled my belt and am outside the car, yanking the back-passenger door open. "Get into the front seat before Neill makes me want to take his head off. Romi, you can at least ride with us into town. We can drop you off before we head to the café." I see she's about to object, but something, and I'm not sure what, makes her change her mind. She rounds the car and gets in behind Neill. I slide into the seat behind Laurence.

I buckle up, biting the inside of my lip so I won't moan when I raise my arm to click the belt into place.

"You okay?" Romi whispers.

"I'm fine." I know she knows I'm lying, but it doesn't matter. "Neill, Laurence," I continue and indicate the guys respectively, "this is Romi." I'm not going to repeat the mistake I made last night when I mentioned the fact that she helped me with some heavy lifting.

"Good to meet you, Romi. We've heard a little bit about you, which is a lot, considering it's tight-lipped Owen doing the talking." Neill smiles broadly through the rearview mirror.

"Nice to meet you." Romi tilts her head at me in a clear challenge. "I can't say I've heard anything about you."

"Touché, Neill," I say triumphantly. "That'll teach you to be a smartass."

"Just kidding, just kidding." Neill lets go of the wheel completely to raise his hands in defeat. It doesn't surprise me at all that Laurence automatically reaches for it and steers the car safely while Neill is being silly. No doubt the more levelheaded Laurence is the reason they haven't experienced the same type of wreck I have. The only reason I can ride in cars without panicking is that I have no memories of my accident. That's what I think, at least. At the hospital I met a man who had yet to set foot in a car more than a year after his wreck. Sure, I've seen photos of my totaled BMW sports car, but it feels as if that's someone else's vehicle. Too surreal, even if my arm is a constant reminder.

"Where are you going?" I now ask Romi, not sure why that matters, but it does. For some reason, ever since the night she passed through my garden, she has gone from being helpful to becoming fascinating.

"I have to do some shopping. There's a new shopping center west of East Quay and—"

"We have time to swing by the shopping center." I know I'm interrupting, but I just know she'll insist on being dropped off close to the marina and will have to walk all the way to the shopping center if I don't take the initiative.

"You sure?" Romi pulls up her cell phone and checks the time. "Okay." Coloring faintly, she wiggles the phone. "I haven't had a cell phone in years, believe it or not. This is pretty cool."

"May I have your number?" I shock myself. And my cheeks grow hot, given the way my words could be received, and I'm sure *are* interpreted, in the front seat by the guys.

"Um. Sure. Absolutely. Give me yours and I'll send you a text." Romi glances at me over her phone. "Can I snap a photo of you to put in my contacts?" Her eyes are sparkling now, and she looks so beautiful that I lose my breath.

"Of course," I say, my voice barely carrying. I hear her phone click right then and feel more vulnerable than I have in years. I manage to give her my number without sounding like a complete madwoman, and soon I get a text from her, which also contains a small photo of her.

"For your contacts," Romi says and shoves her phone back into her pocket, a crooked smile on her lips.

Neill chooses this moment to butt in. "So, Gail tells us you're into music as well."

Romi stiffens next to me, her haunted expression back. "In a manner of speaking. I'm an assistant choir leader. Or I will be tomorrow if all goes well." She presses her palms together and pushes her hands in between her thighs. I get the impression that her fingers instantly went cold right now.

"You'll do fine," I say, sending a murderous glance toward the rearview mirror. Did Neill have to sound like I did nothing but talk incessantly about Romi last night? A thought strikes me. Did I? I think back to us sitting with glasses of red wine and talking until two a.m. Yes. I did mention Romi more than once. Nothing about the awkward moments of physical closeness in the car, but I did let drop little tidbits about her. How careless of me. Neill knows me better than anyone, and I can't imagine, though it's not surprising, that he noticed any tiny, even insignificant, detail I may have let slip last night. I want to groan and clasp my forehead, but naturally, all I do is direct my attention forward and disengage.

After all, I've perfected that skill since that fateful day in the BMW.

CHAPTER TWELVE

Romi

After hurrying out of Gail's friends' car and thanking them for the lift, I stride past the shops in the shopping center. I've already used the brand-new smartphone I got at the store connected to the Belmont Foundation to find the closest camping store in the area. As it turns out, one has recently opened in the new shopping center, and the initial sale is still going on.

I have to get out of Gail's house ASAP, and buying supplies at the camping store is the only way I can think of. I can't say I look forward to sleeping outdoors, but the way I see it, I don't have a choice. If I overhear more tears during confidential talks in the spy corner, I won't be able to live with myself. And who am I trying to fool? Running into Gail seems to be a frequent thing and something I want to be able to do without a shroud of guilt suffocating me.

The camping store is enormous. I pass fishing equipment, clothes for hunting, rifles, literature about any outdoor activity, climbing gear, and then, finally, stuff for campers. I've already spotted a sleeping bag that can tolerate temperatures down to fifteen degrees that's within my budget. Or, rather, it's within range of what cash I have left and still have enough to buy food. I'm going to have to figure out a way to get my nicked preserves from the secret room out of Gail's house, though.

I find the sleeping bag, and to my joy it has been marked down by an additional twenty percent. This means I can buy a solar-powered lantern, an inexpensive backpack meant for kids, and a camping set holding a plate, utensils, a mug—all kept in a plastic storage container. They also have a sale on self-inflatable camping mattresses, and I choose a blue one.

"You're not really thinking of getting that sorry excuse for a backpack?" an amused male voice says from behind, making me jump.

I turn and see a guy my age. He's wearing a shirt that tells me he works in the store and that his name is Ben. "I really just need one to carry my stuff in. I don't care that it says Spidey on it." I shrug.

"Aha. Hmm. Wait. I just can't let you do this. Honestly." Ben shakes his head and rounds the shelf. He returns with a camouflage-patterned backpack three times as big as the Spidey one.

"I can't afford that," I say, squirming inside.

"It's ten bucks more. This is a demo exhibit from our former stores. Surely you can add ten dollars?"

I calculate in my head. Between the cash I earned helping Gail and the advance from Manon—and if I stick to eating from the preserves and an occasional cheeseburger—I can perhaps get it.

"You know what? I'll knock another five bucks off. You'd be helping us get rid of it, actually. That can be worth five dollars." Ben grins at me.

I haven't survived in Manhattan for the last six years by being too proud. "Deal," I say quickly, before he regrets it.

"Fantastic. Let me help you get all this to the checkout. Oh, and by the way, that camping mattress comes with an inflatable pillow. Pretty cool, huh?" Ben's enthusiasm is contagious, and I find myself returning his smile effortlessly. I think he may be flirting with me, and I hope he doesn't think I'm responding on that level.

I adjust my features when we reach the checkout. I count the bills as I place them on the counter, and my stomach is turning, as I have never spent this amount before in one go. Forcing myself to not yank the money back from Ben's hand, I watch him put it in the till and place my items in the backpack.

"There you go," he says, beaming. "Unless there was anything else?"

"Um. No, thank you. This is it. And thanks again for the discount." I accept the backpack and place it over one shoulder.

"Need help adjusting it?" Ben tilts his head, and I know it's time to leave.

"Thanks. I've got it." I nod and walk out of the store. I've lucked out more than I deserve, but I'm not going to stay around long enough for Ben to think I'm *that* grateful.

As I step outside, I find the sun's come out and it's turning into a beautiful day. I figure out the straps of the backpack and put it on. Surprised at how light it feels despite my purchases, I begin walking back toward the farmhouse. If I hurry, I might be able to be out of there, glass jars and all, before Gail and the guys come home.

My new sneakers help the walk seem easier and less cumbersome than usual, and I make good time. I think about what I'll have to buy next time I get paid. Batteries. Yes. And I'll have to be sure I charge my cell phone whenever I'm working or visiting someone. I'll also need one of those cheap coolers. Yes, there's an old, big one in Gail's basement, but I'll be damned if I steal that as well. The food, yes, she won't miss. I admit my reasoning isn't logical as a theft is a theft, but at least I'll be out of her house and not such a creep. All I have to do is remember the time I heard her cry in the spy corner, and my resolve strengthens.

I turn the corner and see the farmhouse, and it's as if my mind splits in two. I see it the way it looked when I lived here with Aunt Clara. Perfectly straight rows of flowers, berry bushes that needed tending to in the summer, fruit trees, the greenhouse, and the entire kitchen garden with vegetables I had to weed. How

I hated it. Not the work per se, even if I was a lazy teenager at times, like most of my peers, but the feeling of not belonging, of being taken for granted as a farmhand and never receiving any praise or recognition. It all made me loathe living here. And now, when Gail lives here and I'm nothing but a trespasser, I can't understand why leaving hurts so badly.

I hurry into the basement and into the bomb shelter. I manage to shove four jars into the backpack, together with the rest of my things. Pretty sure Gail won't notice, or miss, one of Aunt Clara's old shopping bags on wheels, I add the rest and the books from my room. What little I had when I arrived at the farmhouse fits on top of the last jars.

Quickly, I poke my head out the door and listen. No voices. No engine. This is it. I tug on the backpack, which is much heavier now. I pull the bag on wheels after me and push the shelf door closed. Pulling the bag behind me, I drag it up the few steps and then turn around to close the door. My fingers tremble when I hide the key in its usual place. With my entire being, I want to linger, to change my mind, but I can't. As long as I figured I was staying in an uninhabited house, I could justify my presence, but not the way things are.

I pull the bag behind me through the shrubbery, cursing as it keeps getting stuck on the uneven ground. Tears stream down my cheeks now, and I can't quite grasp what I'm about to do. It doesn't matter that I tell myself this will be better than sleeping under a bridge with unstable people as neighbors. At least I'll have a roof over my head. Sort of. It'll still suck. I'll be alone, and it'll only get colder. Yes, today is a great autumn day, but the nights are bitter already.

Sobbing, I chastise myself. I have to get a grip. This is temporary. I have a job, albeit not full-time, but I'll have more money than I've ever had, and I'll be able to save some. After all, I'm used to living on practically nothing. Perhaps I may even be able to rent a room at one point.

If I tell Manon I'm once again homeless, not that I ever was anything else these last few years, she may ask about details, and there are some things I can never share with her—or I'll lose this chance. She must have googled me, and perhaps run a search of me within the state, but if she finds out about the arrest, it won't matter how wrong the accusation was. I'm supposed to be taking care of young kids. Yes, she must've found gaps in my history, naturally, but clearly they haven't been enough for her to have second thoughts. If she thinks I was homeless here in Rhode Island, gaps won't stand out as something unexpected.

Fuck. I'm turning into such a liar. It's true, once you start, one lie leads to another. My stomach lurches again, and when I see the abandoned house appear between the trees and overgrown old garden, I almost drop to my knees and wail.

The front door is half ajar, and I enter carefully, hoping not to find any rodents, skunks, or whatever. Not even cute chipmunks or squirrels. Damn. I don't want to be here.

Making my way into what used to be the living room, I hope it will be in better shape than the kitchen, which is just plain gross. I've been in here twice before, checking it out, and am certain that going up into the attic is not doable. The stairs are rotten, and half the steps are missing.

The living room boasts two wooden chairs and a rickety table that perhaps I can fix. I determine which corner looks less bad than the others and use one of my old T-shirts to sweep away as much of the dust as I can. The sun shines in through barely transparent glass in the only window. It's the only unbroken one in the entire house, which is a blessing, as it will keep rain, and oh, God, snow out.

Now my knees do give in, and I fall sideways down onto one of the chairs, burying my face in my hands. I can't take much more right now, but at least I've done the right thing. Now Gail's house is just that. Her house. No uninvited squatter will be hiding in her basement and lying to her with every breath. When—if—I see her again, I can at least give her that. Her privacy. Her own space no matter which corner, in whatever room, she chooses to sit in.

I drop my hands onto my lap and raise my head. That's it. This is what I need to focus on. Nothing in my life, absolutely nothing, has been more important to me than Gail's well-being. So, what if I need to stay in this near ruin of a house? If I step through the trees in the back, I'll be able to see the lights from her windows. When I walk into East Quay every day, I'll pass her house. Perhaps she'll be outside, and we can say hello. And she knows some of the people I know. I need to cling to these thoughts.

I gaze around me. I have to remain hopeful despite everything, or I'll go crazy. I snort. Perhaps too late for that.

CHAPTER THIRTEEN

Gail

I ache all over and curse that I promised Neill and Laurence I'd find a local physiotherapist. Now I've had my third session at the clinic Manon Belmont recommended, and I've already exchanged the tenacious PT's real name for an unprintable word in my mind. The fact that she seems incredibly capable and doesn't intimidate easily makes me reluctantly impressed and annoyed. She hasn't given me any outlandish promises that I may be able to resume my career in however long, but she's fully convinced that I'll regain normal use of my arm—and that the pain situation will get better. Right now, I doubt it, as my entire arm throbs and aches to a degree that I had to hit the bathroom to wipe my eyes and blow my nose.

"Gail?"

I stop and pivot as a familiar voice says my name softly from behind me. Romi. Now, it's not my arm that's the problem, but my stomach that clenches so tight, the sensation is close to pain. I haven't seen Romi in ten days. Not since the guys and I drove her to that shopping center. She hasn't taken the shortcut through my yard on her way home, or at least not as far as I've seen.

"Romi. Heading to your house?" I cradle the sling around my orthosis awkwardly, but she doesn't even look at my arm. Instead her huge, hazel eyes gaze firmly into mine.

"Yes. I've been at the Belmont Center. With the kids." She tugs at a fabric messenger bag. "We're practicing for a local competition." Romi shifts and turns her focus onto her feet.

Thinking fast, I try to figure out a way to keep her around a little longer. "I'm due for some grocery shopping. Can I persuade you to tag along? I mean, if you don't have anywhere else you need to be?"

Gazing up again, Romi gives a faint smile. "I'm free for today. I don't mind coming with you." She looks at the building I just exited and frowns. "You all right?"

"I'm fine. Just PT." I want to shrug, but that's always painful, no matter which shoulder, really. "I'm parked over there." I point at the parking lot to the left of the building.

In the car, Romi extends her hand toward my seat belt without my having to ask. At some point, on a particularly grumpy day, I would have thought she was being presumptuous, but today I'm merely grateful. It's as if she simply gets it and makes absolutely no fuss about my handicap.

I drive toward the Whole Foods Market not far from the shopping center, where we dropped her off that Sunday. "What music is the choir planning to perform?" I ask when the silence starts to get to me.

"It appears that the kids really liked the song they heard me sing and wanted to perform another one from the same musical, 'This Is Me.' At first, Carrie, their leader, thought it was too hard for the girls, but they insisted. As it turned out, they're really good." Romi raises her thumb to her lips and nibbles at it for a moment but then yanks it away. "I'm worried, though. Next week, Carrie's going to have surgery, and I'm sort of going to be it. I've only been the assistant three times. I may screw everything up." She sighs. "Sorry."

Glancing furtively at her, I can tell she's pushed her shoulders up. "For what?"

"Didn't mean to dump all that on you." Romi presses her

palms together and hides her hands between her thighs in a, by now, familiar gesture.

"You did nothing of the sort." I infuse some of my work voice, wanting, well, not to intimidate her, of course, but for her to know that I don't mind hearing anything she'd feel comfortable sharing. Not being the smoothest communicator in the world, I fully expect to be misunderstood. "And I think those girls are lucky to have you, especially since their original leader isn't well. This way they don't have to miss any rehearsals."

"Thanks." Romi's shoulders sink slowly, and she exhales.

"Here we are." I pull into the grocery-store parking lot.

"Oh, God."

"What? What's wrong?" I park the car and turn to Romi, who looks oddly dismayed.

"N-nothing. Nothing at all." Romi presses the release to my belt and eases it carefully up across my chest until I can catch it with my good arm. "I'll go grab a cart, okay?"

"Okay." Mystified, I make my way out of the car. Every time I think I have a grip on my situation with Romi, she says or does something that makes me feel utterly confused. Not in an unpleasant way, not at all, really, but in a way that makes me think I've been missing out on social interaction one-on-one since I was a toddler. Or perhaps I've simply happened upon a young woman who challenges me into truly wanting to interpret her feelings and motives. Understand her.

And if this isn't enough, her physical closeness totally bewilders me. She's not my type. She's too young. She's wrong in so many ways. Still, ever since that evening after the dinner at Vivian and Mike's, something about Romi has been…if not right, exactly, then, not entirely incorrect.

Exasperated at myself, I watch Romi return with a shopping cart. She tilts her head questioningly at me, but I motion for her to keep pushing it. This gesture makes her light up, for some reason, and she walks next to me with what I feel is a new bounce in her step. Last time I saw her, she was definitely under a thundercloud, and I barely felt connected, but now, as ghostly thin as she seems, Romi seems happier.

We walk up and down the aisles, and I pick out the fruit and vegetables I want, my favorite coffee, cocoa, and tea. Yes, I like to spoil myself, or should I say, I used to like it. Ever since the accident, I've gone through the motions, bought my usual stuff, but not really cared. Now, in Romi's presence, I feel a certain satisfaction in choosing what I really enjoy, and before I realize where my brain is heading, I envision us having hot chocolate by the fireplace. The thought makes me come to a dead stop and stare at Romi's back as she pushes the cart along the aisle without noticing I'm not beside her—but for only three steps.

"Gail?" She looks over her shoulder and then returns to me. This part of her, this protective side, should drive me up the wall like it does with anyone else that I fear might pity me. Romi doesn't pity me, she just seems to—care.

"I'm fine. Just trying to remember what else to get." I lie to save my sanity, but she takes my words at face value, or seems to, as she looks up and down the aisle. "More coffee?"

"Um. No. Actually, I need a coffee grinder. I like freshly ground beans." I manage a flippant tone.

Romi crinkles her nose. "Thank God. I was afraid you were going to say you chew them whole, or something."

I laugh, and it's such an alien feeling, I have to fight a burning sensation along my lower eyelids. When did I burst into laughter last? I can't remember, but an educated guess would be before the accident, though I've never been the giggly type. I'm sure my peers think I'm pretty humorless.

"Heaven forbid—that's not for me." I start walking and we round the shelf.

Now it's Romi's turn to stop. "Whoa. Look at these cereals. Never seen them packaged like that. And the mixes!" Her eyes are even bigger than usual when she turns to me.

"Why don't you get some now that you have a ride?"

Leaning closer to the shelf, reading the price tags, Romi shakes her head. "Not in my price range. Too bad. Perhaps another time." She shrugs and seems completely unaffected. "I don't mind a regular box of corn flakes."

I'm half a second away from offering to buy her some of the pricey cereals when I realize what a horrible mistake—and how condescending—such a suggestion might seem to Romi. I merely keep walking, and once we've been through all the aisles, I've even found my coffee grinder. It seems easy to use with one hand, which is a relief.

After we check out, and Romi and the young man carrying out my groceries have stowed everything in the back of my car, I motion at the passenger seat. "Now that you've pushed my cart and packed up everything, please let me make you dinner. And before you say it's not necessary, I have ulterior motives. I need someone to chop some vegetables." I know I've played dirty, as I could tell Romi had an excuse ready to go.

"Thank you. I don't have a chance to eat much home-cooked food." Romi gets into the car and I join her. As has started to become a habit, she extends her hand for my safety belt once I pull it toward my right. She attaches it, ever mindful of my right arm.

"It's not a gourmet meal," I say as I pull out of the parking lot. "Just a casserole with mainly vegetables and some chicken."

"You're kidding, right? Sounds like gourmet food to me." Smiling easily now, sitting slightly turned toward me, Romi is the most relaxed I've ever seen her. Oddly, this makes her look more mature, even a little self-assured. Is this the real Romi who hides behind the young woman with haunted eyes and tense body language?

I drive through the bright autumn afternoon and reach the house just as the sun begins to set. It's getting darker earlier and earlier, and I used to love this time of the year. I was never much for summer, with all its outdoor activities I felt I should adore. Sitting on my couch in my condo, reading, listening to music, or even occasionally watching TV, with some candles burning and a fire going, is much more my thing. That said, being a professional musician, I needed physical stamina to deliver the performances in the manner that I expected of myself. I preferred my local gym rather than running in Central Park, like some of my peers did. Treadmills, ellipticals, rowing machines were my equipment of choice. Much less risk of tripping and injuring my—well, as it turned out, all I had to do was get behind the wheel of my car and have someone else run a red light in Midtown.

"You're frowning again? Still hurting from the PT?" Romi asks, interrupting my darkening thoughts.

"Yes." It's not a lie, but not the entire truth, of course. "I suppose it's that type of situation when it has to get worse before it gets better."

"Wish those pesky worse parts would let up a bit more often—for all of us." Romi shrugs. "And I hate to see you in pain."

"You do?" I groan inwardly about speaking before I engaged my brain. Of course, she would hate to see anyone in pain, hardly just me.

"Yes. It's not just the physical part, but how the pain seems to affect...um...more of you." Romi's cheekbones turn pink, or perhaps it's the glow of the setting sun. "That sounds damn presumptuous. Sorry."

"Don't apologize. I appreciate the insight." I drum the fingers of my left hand against the wheel. "To be honest, I normally loathe any type of so-called insight, or any attempt at 'reaching me.' Especially after...this." I lift my arm a fraction of an inch. "It's amazing how much unsolicited advice people who barely know you can offer in one sitting."

Romi seems to consider this remark for a moment. "People mean well." Her tone is noncommittal, and I guess she's been on the receiving end of that sentence more than once. "Even when they walk right over your soul and try to yank you off the ground at the same time, whether you want to or not, they still only mean well. When you try to protect yourself by keeping them at a distance, they sure can make you feel guilty. Perhaps we really need help, need to be yanked up, but just because we've fallen doesn't mean we don't have our own will, our own hopes and dreams. Our own way of wanting to do things. That's when they go from meaning well to letting us know that beggars can't be choosers." She looks at me with worried eyes.

"I hear you," I say softly. And I do. These aren't just words. She's talking about her reality, which clearly differs from mine, but the sentiment is the same. "I really do."

"Okay. Cool." Romi turns forward again, but I can see a faint smile come and go on her lips.

We drive back to the house in silence, and this time it's comfortable. As we come up the driveway, Romi unbuckles her belt and turns toward me again, ready to assist with my belt as if it's no big deal—just something she does. A fire ignites in my chest at this thought, warming with its soft glow rather than scorching me. Oh, I don't doubt she could burn me to a crisp if I ever let her that close, but in this instant and for the first time in ages, Romi makes me feel safe.

CHAPTER FOURTEEN

Romi

The chicken casserole is among the best I've ever tasted. Looking up at Gail, I confess that her presence is the main reason for the way everything tastes. She sits there, still looking like her stern self, probably second nature to her, but unless my imagination is going nuts, she's smiled at me three times since we sat down. That has to be a record.

I hope the damn soap I've used ever since I moved out isn't too obvious. Of all things to worry about, and God knows I have a few, this is ridiculous. At least I know how to get to work clean. The gas station located in the outskirts of East Quay is conveniently on my way as I walk into town. Their restrooms are well kept and provide all the free soap I need. That said, I plan to make my way to one of the cheaper stores in East Quay and buy a better soap. My hair is blissfully short and easy to wash in the sink, but I hate how it feels when washed with cheap hand soap. Then again, at least I'm clean.

"I'm glad you're enjoying the chicken." Gail puts her fork down and dabs her lips with a paper napkin. "Up for dessert? I have ice cream."

Of course, true to my habit, I've wolfed down the food, despite my best intentions. I'm so full now, I'm ready to burst, no matter how delicious some ice cream would be. "Sorry, but I have to pass. The casserole was so good, I overate."

"We can always wait a bit. Unless you're in a hurry to go home?" Gail gets up and places her plate in the dishwasher. The machine is brand-new, which makes sense since Aunt Clara didn't believe in redundant appliances. I washed a lot of dishes by hand, which was one of my chores I didn't mind. Perhaps it sounds nuts, but I found the warm water against my hands soothing. Compared to the drying nature of the soil in the flower and vegetable beds, it was almost pleasurable. I know how pathetic this sounds, even to myself, and force my brain to change gears.

"Romi?" Gail rests her hip against the counter and regards me with a deepening frown. I realize she's still waiting for an answer and scramble my scattering thoughts to try to remember what she asked just now. Ah. Yes.

"No, I'm not in a hurry. I don't have to be at work until after lunch tomorrow." I pick up my plate and place it and my glass in the dishwasher. "Thanks again. Dinner was good."

Gail nods. "Why don't you go into the living room? I'll be there in a moment."

"All right." I walk into the room where Aunt Clara spent every evening by the fire—mending, knitting, or listening to the radio. I sometimes felt as if I lived in the forties, before the television era. I got to watch TV at a friend's house once in a while, and when I raised the subject of getting one, Aunt Clara would huff and shake her finger at me, assuring me that such a redundant device would never cross her threshold. Honestly, I think Aunt Clara used the word "redundant" every day.

I hear Gail walk back to the downstairs bathroom and close the door. Scanning the living room, I immediately see the huge flat-screen. Aunt Clara must be spinning in her grave, poor woman. She was so adamant, but now, with a new owner living among her things, no doubt exchanging them little by little, everything is different.

I sit on the couch across from the TV and can't stop myself.

Gail will probably think me too forward and rather presumptuous, but I grab the remote and turn it on. The TV is set to a cooking channel, which is sort of surprising, but after having Gail's home-cooked chicken casserole, it shouldn't be.

"I see you found my latest purchase. They delivered it two days ago." Gail comes into the living room and sits down next to me on the couch.

I nearly choke, as I haven't been this close to her outside the car. No, that's not right. She was really close to me when I fell in the basement. But this is still different. She had the choice of the armchair or the old rocker when she came in, but she chose to sit right next to me. Not even at the opposite end of the couch but up close and personal. Jesus. I clutch the remote while trying to think of something to say. "It's impressive," I manage to say, my voice too low and trembly. "Don't think I've ever watched anything on such a big set." Who am I kidding? I haven't watched TV outside of electronic stores the last six years. I've been at libraries, using computers and reading papers and magazines, but never watched real television.

"Sixty inches. I figured I might as well get a proper size since there's little else to do at night here in the sticks. I mean, I read a lot nowadays, sure, but it can get a little...quiet." Gail turns to me, raising her bent left arm up on the backrest, resting her head in her hand. "I don't mind if we have the TV on, not at all, but can we turn the sound down, so we can talk? With you here, it seems a waste—" She stops, her cheeks going pink.

"I agree." Pressing the mute button on the remote, I mimic her and turn slightly toward her on the couch. There's something so very rare about being under the unwavering scrutiny of Gail Owen. Her eyes, so bright, so damn blue, can go from ice to a warm, almost turquoise hue in seconds. Right now, they're definitely the latter, and they pull me in.

In moments like this, Gail can easily convince me to confide all my secrets to her. My poor heart wants nothing more than to unburden my guilt for trespassing, for lying about my past, for—being me. I'd give anything for her to hear the truth and still look at me with such warmth. Does Gail, who normally is so standoffish, realize how far she's dropped her guard with me? It's been gradual, but it's also been quick. No doubt it wouldn't take much for her to pull back into her shell again—and speaking of shells, how the hell am I going to find a way out of my own?

"Any topics in mind for us?" Gail smiles faintly.

"It depends." I really would hate to sit here and suffer through some small talk that we'd both loathe. "I mean, it depends on whether you're comfortable talking about real stuff or not."

"Define 'real stuff.'" Gail frowns, but the warmth is still there.

"You know. Not the weather, latest Kardashian drama, who's up for an Oscar..." I chuckle when Gail manages to look affronted.

"Is that what you think I normally discuss?" she asks, raising her left eyebrow in a way that makes my thighs clench all on their own.

"No, but you're a private person. That's pretty obvious." I follow the seam on the thighs of my new jeans back and forth with my index finger.

"And accurate. And the same goes for you. I don't think we're all that different in some ways. We don't like it when people ask too many questions—at least neither of us did during the dinner party." Gail's gaze falls to my hand, and I see her swallow hard. What the hell? Why is she staring at...? Oh, shit. I'm an idiot. Not only that. A dense idiot. But how could I possibly even begin to imagine that Gail would ever look at me that way? Even for a *second*? What the hell am I going to do? Say? Should I just play it cool and pretend I didn't just see a very clear sign that Gail's not entirely straight and that she's not indifferent to me?

I can hardly breathe, and of course my body, my poor, inexperienced body, is ready to throw itself at the woman who is so far out of my league, she could live on another planet.

"Romi? Where did you go?" Gail lets her left hand fall onto my shoulder, shaking me gently.

"I, um…I…" I cough in a ridiculous attempt to find something reasonably coherent to say. No such luck. "I'm sorry." Remembering my words earlier about talking about real stuff, I dig for courage. "It's just, well, the way you look at me. Can't blame a girl for losing her train of thought." I gaze at Gail, who now either will pull back or very kindly tell me I'm imagining things on a pathological level.

"Dear God." Slumping back, Gail stares at me, and I can't decipher her expression. "I'm really not in my regular form, am I?"

I get that it's a rhetorical question and keep my mouth shut.

"Should I apologize?" Gail raises her chin in a clear challenge, but I recognize that gesture. She's donning her armor, or she will, if I say the wrong thing.

"Never." Not sure where my courage comes from, and I'm pretty sure this is a do-or-die moment, I run the back of my fingers along her cheek. "I promise. Not to me."

Gail's eyes have detoured to the icy blue but now warm marginally again. "Good."

Trying to will my body to cool off, since it's pretty clear that the earlier snippet of mutual desire is over for now, I pull one leg up and hug my knee to my chest. Aunt Clara would have berated me for having my feet up on the couch, but I somehow know Gail won't care. I need the barrier of my leg between us, or my simmering arousal will reignite.

"Things can sure take a turn when you least expect it," Gail murmurs and resumes her earlier position.

"Tell me about it." Relieved that we're just talking again, I nod. "I sure never would've guessed that moving back to Rhode Island would put me in your path—and Manon Belmont's. To get a job is—miraculous."

"Did you lose your job in New York?" Tilting her head back into her hand, Gail looks at me unwaveringly.

"Sort of, yes. Coming back here was my best option." I've promised myself not to add to my previous lies, but I know I'm skidding along the edge of fabrication.

"When did you leave East Quay?"

"When I was sixteen." The truth flies out of me before I realize it. "I was too young, really."

"Sixteen?" Gail's eyes grow bigger. "And your parents agreed to this?"

"I was orphaned when I was very little. I grew up with a relative." I hope we'll brush over this part of my life fast. I know I'll trip and fall if I have to involve my aunt.

"And you've moved back in with them now?"

Fuck. "Not per se. I'm staying at a house close to their property." Damn it, this isn't going well. I'm going to slip up, and Gail's going to guess the truth, and she's going to—

"I'm sorry. I didn't mean to give you the third degree." Holding her hand up as if in surrender, Gail shakes her head. "I suppose I'm quite curious about you. No, wrong word. Interested." Again, her cheeks color faintly, and I wonder if she's always been this transparent, but I don't think so. Until the evening after the dinner party I've thought of Gail as completely opaque, as encased in glass. Now, it's as if her facade has partly… not cracked, really, but melted. This woman, looking younger for sure, with her radiant eyes and glowing complexion, is Gail, but not the woman I met when she first moved in.

"Romi?" Looking concerned again, Gail briefly touches my knee, making me jump. "Hey. You disappeared again."

"Sorry." I've got to stop doing this but have no idea how. Everything about Gail takes so much energy, and my mind struggles to process it all. The fact that it takes a while doesn't help.

"So, you have a rehearsal tomorrow. How do you like being a choir leader?" Gail seems as ready as I am to change the subject.

"I like it. I mean, I don't consider myself a true choir director. I don't have any formal education when it comes to music.

Autodidact, that's me. Which in my present company seems very fake, somehow." I shrug awkwardly.

"Music isn't just for the ones who've attended conservatories. Yes, I spent all my free time from age seven until eighteen months ago practicing my violin. I sacrificed a lot and it was worth it. Until—" Gail sighs.

"Until eighteen months ago," I say softly. "And when something life-changing like that happens, it makes you question everything." I rub my neck, suddenly feeling so tired and low at the thought of how my life has changed and the cold, half-collapsed house I have to return to.

"Yes. Exactly that." Tilting her head again, Gail studies me closely. "What happened to change your life? I mean, first here and then in New York? You don't have to answer. As I said, you interest me." She sounds baffled.

"When I was sixteen, I ran away. I couldn't take it anymore, and the situation on the home front wasn't great. So, I had saved up and left for New York, which turned out to be an expensive place." I stop there, unsure how to continue.

"What happened when you got there?" Gail gently rubbed the outside of her sling.

"I—wait. You're in pain again. I've definitely overstayed my welcome. I should go."

"What—wait." Gail straightens as I begin to get up. "Dessert?"

"I'm going to have to take a rain check." I can barely speak now; my voice is trembling. I make my way to the hallway and fumble for my jacket, where it hangs next to Gail's. "I'm really grateful for dinner." I force the words out so fast, they nearly leave my mouth in the wrong order. Gail has followed me to the front door.

"Wait. Please." She holds her good arm protectively around her sling. "Tell me you're not leaving because I said something wrong." Her expression is so vulnerable, my heart aches, and I know I can't leave her with her feeling like that.

"You didn't do anything wrong. I really need to get home."
Home. What a joke. Even the cardboard I spent months sleeping in was homier than the ruin I'm returning to now.

Gail comes closer, stepping well within my personal space. I lose what little breath I have left. She lets go of her aching arm and instead cups my cheek, whisper-light. Her touch levels the last of my resolve. My self-control, which I've paid so dearly for during the years I've struggled to survive, crumbles.

Placing my hand over Gail's, I hold it firmly against my cheek. These are precious, precious seconds that will never come again. Gail's touching me. She's concerned about me, and right now I'm the only one she sees. I soak up the amazing feelings, eager for them to permeate me and become one with the fabric of who I am.

"Come with me to practice tomorrow?" I hear myself say, and for some unfathomable reason, my words seem to be the right ones. Gail's eyes grow turquoise again, her fingers move against my skin in tiny circles, and she smiles.

Leaning in, she presses her lips to my other cheek, lingering only a moment. "All right. Just come knocking and I'll be ready."

I want nothing more than to press my lips to hers, but of course I don't. She wants to see me again. My heart does something that feels like crazy pirouettes. "Around one p.m."

"See you then." Gail lets go of my cheek, and I pull on my jacket.

As I step out into the crisp evening, not even the walk across Gail's yard toward the abandoned house can wipe the smile off my face. Yes, yes. I'm not crazy. Nothing can come of this. Naturally, I know this. Sooner or later, Gail will discover the truth about me. This means I need to log as many Gail-hours as possible. I need them to last me a lifetime.

CHAPTER FIFTEEN

Gail

I watch Romi walk out the door, and the noise the deadbolt makes when I lock it behind her mimics the pang in my heart. Why does it bother me   no, not just bother me, *hurt* me, to see her walk away? I don't know this young woman. Not really. The thoughts barely flicker through my brain before my entire being objects. Yes, I *do* know her. On some miraculous level, I know Romi, and I can't for the life of me figure out how that's possible. She's secretive. So am I, though I think we're on completely different levels. Romi is guarded. Me too. Though I wasn't this evening.

I make my way upstairs after turning off most of the lights on the bottom floor. Walking into the bathroom, I look longingly at the tub but settle for running the shower. I'm very tired and fear I may fall asleep in the bathtub again. Removing the sling, I slowly extend my injured arm, using the joint of the orthosis like the physiotherapist showed me. It's damn sore, but not *as* sore as it was after my first appointment here in East Quay. Perhaps Manon was right when she recommended this PT?

The orthosis is attached with strips of Velcro, which I remove carefully. When the air reaches my skin, I can see and feel goose bumps form on it. I shudder, and a glance in the mirror shows the two scars, paler now, but still red and ugly. The first, six inches long, is located at my wrist. The one at my elbow is only four inches, but it hurts the most. I shake my head at the evidence that my life was literally over when that man ran a red light and slammed into my BMW. I have no idea at what angle he hit me, to make the wheel twist and break my right arm so badly. In many ways I'm grateful that I have no memory of the accident, but I still have questions that only the man hitting me can answer. I grit my teeth. No way in hell will I ever reach out to him. The police gave me a reasonably accurate version of what they thought occurred and what the other driver told them. They said he was in a state of shock but physically unharmed, as he was driving an SUV. I suppose my little Beemer had no chance against his vehicle.

The shower soothes me, it always does, and I've grown accustomed to lathering up using only one hand. My new PT told me I need to work on developing muscle tone in my injured arm, as it has lost a lot of muscle tissue from being inactive too long. I tried to explain how incompetent I'd found my former PTs, not to mention the first surgeons, but this new woman—what was her name again? Yvette? Annette?—refused to let me get away with casting blame elsewhere. She insisted that if I was unhappy about my PT, I should have found someone I could work with instead of sitting around the house and uselessly licking my wounds. I'll never know how she managed to tell me this in such a friendly manner that I couldn't snarl at her like I wanted to.

Stepping out of the shower, I dry off and slip into my sleep T-shirt. I loathe nightgowns or full pajamas. Long men's T-shirts are perhaps a bit tricky to get into, but if I slide my bad arm in first, I can usually wriggle into one without too much hassle. After brushing my teeth, I walk toward the bedroom. Passing the door to one of the spare rooms I have yet to redo, I stop, suddenly curious. If I remember correctly, this room once belonged to a kid.

I push the door open and switch on the ceiling light, and the dust whirls up a bit. The furniture is mostly covered with sheets, but I gently pull them off, mindful of not inhaling or touching the dust. A worn desk comes into view. It's almost eerie to see the writing pads, stickers, pens, coloring pens, and other items sitting there as if waiting for their owner to return any moment. A single bed with a pink bedspread stretches along the far wall. I tug away the last sheet covering a bookshelf filled with books, some young-adult ones and some kids' books. I remove one. After reading the back cover, I realize it's a romance novel for teenagers. I put it back and pull out five more, reading the back blurb and flipping through some pages. So, whoever lived here was fond of reading. Then something catches my eyes. On one of the lower shelves, the dust that has snuck in under the sheet has been disturbed. In six different places, it looks like books are missing. How the hell did that happen? If it had taken place before I moved in, it would have grown dusty again, right?

Frowning, I try to solve the mystery, but I really am exhausted and want to curl up with a good book of my own. I turn to leave, but one of the book spines gives off a sparkle, and I can't resist pulling it out. "*Goodnight Mister Tom.*" I jump as I read the title out loud. I was always a reader, even if my love of books had to take a back seat since playing my violin always came first for me. My grandmother gave me a first edition of this book at Christmas one year, I think I was fourteen, and told me it was published the year after I was born. For some reason this fact stuck in my memory, and when I lost that book along with an entire crate when moving into my penthouse in Manhattan, I felt as if I'd lost my grandmother all over again. Seeing the book now, in pristine condition, makes me tremble.

I open it and see something written on the inside of the cover.

This book belongs to RS. I paid for it myself. Allegedly I've mowed lawns across half of freaking East Quay, but in truth, busking's the name of the game.

Busking? I snort in disbelief. Whoever the original owner was, it's mine now, according to the contract I signed with the representative of the seller. "Poor RS. You should have taken it with you. Oh, well." I tuck the book under my left arm and walk into my bedroom.

Only a small lamp on my nightstand is lit, but it's enough. Placing the book there, I move over to the window to close the blinds. I look out into the late-evening darkness, not expecting to see anything but perhaps a passing car's headlights out on the main road. Instead I see a faint, flickering light in the opposite direction. This is the first time I've noticed any light over there. Is that where Romi's staying? If so, why haven't I seen anything from that part of the neighborhood until now? Perhaps it's because the leaves have fallen a lot more the last couple of days?

I try to judge how far away the house is located, but it's impossible to guess in the dark. I suppose it could be about four hundred yards, give or take. I remain by the window until I start to shiver, Romi on my mind again. As I crawl into bed, I realize I've forgotten the orthosis in the bathroom and have to return to collect it. I can't sleep without it, no matter how uncomfortable it is. If I should accidentally move my injured arm under my body…it has happened before, and I don't want to even think about how much that hurt. I screamed so loud, I was sure my neighbors in Manhattan would call the police.

Finally in bed, I take *Goodnight Mister Tom* and open the cover again. The acerbic note is written with an adolescent handwriting, but at least not adorned with hearts or stars. I begin to read, but every time I turn the page, I think of Romi. Those warm, apprehensive hazel eyes. Her pale, nearly transparent skin, and, oh God, that soft, apricot-colored mouth…and barely-there freckles. If I had a type, which I don't think I do, Romi would certainly not be it.

Perhaps this is why I'm so uncharacteristically bewildered. The last lover I had, and I cringe at how long ago that was, was an accomplished musician like myself. What a disaster. We were both self-absorbed, ambitious, and yes, competitive, people. Even in bed. The sex could be great, but no greater than my trusty vibrator. When I realized this fact, and that the woman who shared my bed and my professional life would never do more than that for me, I broke it off, and she wasn't any more upset than if she'd lost her cell phone. Annoyed, yes. I suppose it was convenient to have a friend with benefits who understood what it was like to be a professional musician at our level.

I hug the book closer. No way can I even contemplate Romi in the same light as that woman. Before her, I'd had short relationships with men, some of them very nice, but so wrong for me—as I found out. Now, as I picture Romi by my front door, her hand holding mine to her cheek, her eyes probing me with such concern and care, I tremble. And to be completely honest, the vision of her makes my stomach clench. I haven't felt this aroused in…oh, God, *years*. Then I start to laugh and sob at the same time.

When I came to this house in the sticks, I didn't even pack my fucking vibrator.

Romi

The house is colder than ever before. Probably because I just left the warmth of Gail's home. The contrast is staggering. I make my way into the living-room area and turn on the LED lantern. I'm going to have to take it with me to charge tomorrow, however that's going to work out. As Gail's coming with me, which I'm so nervous and giddy about, I can barely think. Will she find it super strange that I charge a lamp in the office area? I'll just have to make sure the kids distract her enough that she won't see what I'm up to.

I open the little cooler, which is more to keep rodents and other animals away from my stash of food than to keep anything cold. I take a vitamin pill, a force of habit from being homeless so long. An old guy once told me it was what kept him going when the food was scarce and far between.

I sip from my water. I have to find a way to top up the container somehow, but I'm so tired right now, I can't think of an obvious way.

I change into my soft sweatshirt and use the last of the water in my cup to brush my teeth just outside the door. The night sky is cloudless, and the stars and the moon light up the overgrown garden. Returning inside, I make sure the makeshift alarm system I devised from some threads I pulled from some ratty old curtains hanging in the kitchen and empty cans is set in place. If a large animal or, worse, some stranger, enters through any of the broken windows or the rickety door, I'll hear them. I sleep with a knife under my pillow.

The sleeping bag warms me quickly, and I burrow into it much like the animals I just thought of. I wrap my arms around myself and wish they were Gail's. Wincing, I try to push that thought away, knowing the futility of such dreams. Dreams are double-edged swords that slice into you in the night, when you dare to indulge in wishful thinking. I can't count the times I've cursed myself back to front for hoping and wishing for something I know will never come true.

At times I think of a home of my own, of friends, of simple pleasures like watching TV…and the ultimate wish, someone to love and who will love me back. That desire, that yearning, has surfaced since I came back to East Quay, and now I know the exact moment the wall crumbled. Right there on Gail's driveway, as shocked as I was at seeing someone move in to Aunt Clara's house, was the instant my heart leaped and began freefalling.

I curl up on my side and whimper. There's just no hope. My past is a weedy airfield where my growing emotions regarding Gail will crash and burn. Then there's the fact that we come from vastly different worlds. She has money, is world renowned, and when her arm has healed, she will move on to bigger, better things. Gail may not be able to play the violin like the virtuoso she used to be, but she'll find something to compensate for that part—and that won't, can't, be me.

Trying to calm myself, I rock back and forth in the sleeping bag, the faint rustling from the movement soothing me. In my treacherous mind that won't stop dreaming, and thus hoping, Gail's arms are around me, and she's keeping us both warm as she breathes against the back of my neck. I close my eyes, inhale her scent, so vivid and clear, and I swear I can hear her whisper my name just before I fall asleep.

CHAPTER SIXTEEN

Gail

I gaze up at the sky as I step out of the car. We're at the parking lot belonging to the Belmont Foundation Center, where Romi works with the young people in the choir. The modern structure is designed to fit in with the old New England town, which speaks to Manon's attachment to it. I tip my head back and examine the shingled exterior. It consists of three floors holding offices, conference rooms, auditoriums, and studios, all meant to be used to help the less privileged in our society.

I already regret joining Romi in this endeavor, and if I had been able to find a good enough excuse, I would've bailed out on her. But who am I kidding? When I saw her standing by my car as I exited the house, any reasons I could conjure up disappeared from my mind. Instead I felt myself smile as I walked toward her. The fact that she smiled right back was enough to make my breath catch.

"Ready to come inside?" Romi asks, interrupting my musings.

"Sure." I walk next to her, suddenly so nervous, and I can't for the life of me figure out why. Is it because I'll be around young people, who are not part of my usual social circle? Or is it because music will be today's theme? Probably both.

The lobby isn't made of the cold marble, glass, and brass that public-building architects are so fond of. Instead I see dark hardwood flooring, wallpapered walls, and several groups of couches and armchairs, all with their own area rug. It looks like an extended living-room area. Magazines, several fireplaces, books, board games—but no television sets, I note as I take in the setup and the people hanging out. The people are of all ages, and some are engaged in discussion while others are reading. Very few seem mesmerized by their cell phones, which seems to be the norm these days.

"We sign in over here." Romi nudges my left arm and points to the reception area, which is the smallest part of the lobby.

The girl behind the counter can't be more than seventeen or eighteen. She smiles broadly toward Romi as she pulls out guest badges for us both. "Nice to see you again, Romi. Ms. Belmont said that once your paperwork clears, you'll get your permanent badge."

I hear a small gasp from Romi, and my eyes snap up to look at her. Her normally alabaster complexion is now even whiter than usual. I don't want to draw attention to her paleness in front of the other young woman but take a step closer to Romi. "All set?"

"Yeah." Romi nods at the girl and then leads me to the elevators.

"What's the matter?" I ask in a low voice as we step inside the closest one.

"What? Oh, nothing. I'm fine." Romi presses the button for the second floor. It's clearly a lie.

"You're as white as a ghost, and that happened just now. At the counter." I place two fingers under Romi's chin and gently tip her head back. "You're going to face your choir in mere minutes, and you can't go in looking like this."

"Fuck. You're right." Romi closes her eyes hard. "I need—I need a minute."

The elevator stops, and I exit. "Restroom?" I spot a sign two doors down.

"Not the one here. The girls are all in there before we start. There's a smaller one around the corner for the staff." Romi's voice is husky now, and I get the feeling she's trying hard not to cry.

"Come on, then."

We turn a corner and see the sign indicating the staff restroom. Luckily, it's empty. I check the door after we're inside and find it locks even if there are individual stalls inside. I turn the deadbolt. Looking over my shoulder at Romi, I find her holding on to one of the sinks, her eyes closed. She's trembling, and I act without really considering the consequences. I run some cold water in the sink next to her and dampen a paper towel. Squeezing it, I nudge Romi's shoulder with the back of my hand. She faces me slowly, and I notice that her kajal has smudged some, and tears have made faint gray tracks on her pale cheeks.

"Allow me." I gently wipe her cheeks. "Look up." She obeys, and I dab at the smudged parts. "There you go. Less panda." I toss the paper towel into the bin. "Better?"

"Yes. And no." Romi's eyes are still wide, and she makes me think of a cornered animal. I can't for the life of me guess what triggered this, well, panic attack, I suppose. We were at the counter, everything was fine until… I think back to what the girl in the reception said. Something about Romi getting a permanent badge. Wait. After Romi's paperwork cleared. That was it—it had to be.

"Is there something in your past that might jeopardize your new job?" Even I can hear how uncharacteristically gentle I sound.

"Oh, God." Romi sags to the side, supporting herself against the sink. "Yes, there is. I'm fucked," she whispers. "I might as well go to her office and tell her I can't stay." She lifts her gaze to me, and the devastation on her face slowly morphs into resignation.

"Hold on. Don't jump the gun here. And stop panicking." I cup her chin, much like how I touched her face last night. "Before you do that, why don't you and I brainstorm about it?"

Huffing, Romi straightens, but she allows me to hold on to her. "You're telling me you want to help, when you have no clue about my past?" She's challenging me, but not so much that I can't see the pain and confusion behind her bravado.

"I'm not big on trust these days," I say lightly, "but it can't be a secret that I care…what happens to you." I come damn close to saying "care about you," but I don't want to go that far yet.

"No. No secret. And that goes both ways." Romi takes a deep breath. "I just can't see how—"

"Do you think I'd lie to you?" I take a step closer, which leaves only a few inches between us. Letting go of her chin, I move my hand up and brush an errant tear from the highest point of her right cheekbone.

"No." The immediate answer makes me feel soft inside, and the emotion is so rare, I slide my hand to the back of Romi's neck. I run my thumb in an unplanned caress behind the delicate shell of her ear, which makes her shiver.

"Well, then. Time to go to work. You still have to reassure me that these cool young people won't mind having an old woman visiting them." I let go of her and give my best impression of a suffering look.

Romi snorts and shakes her head. "Old, huh? Not likely." Glancing at her reflection in the mirror, she nods. "All right. Panic postponed. Let's go."

Romi

It's funny and interesting to watch the interaction between Gail and my choir kids. Well, kids and kids. Some of them are only five years younger than me, but most of them are still in middle school or junior high.

Gail keeps a low profile at first, sitting on a chair just inside the door, but it's obvious that her elegance and, yes, beauty, make the kids curious. As Carrie isn't here, I'm the one in charge, and I've already learned that nothing gets everyone's attention faster than a wolf whistle. It's something I'm really good at, fortunately. I stick two fingers into my mouth and blow, hard and fast. The kids all turn to me, which is what I expect. Watching Gail's eyes widen is even better.

I take the choir through the first two verses of "This Is Me," stopping them every so often to make them listen to the lyrics and emote the feelings in the song. A few of the girls have a problem following the melody, and when we attempt it a fourth time and they still come in early, or if I stop them in time, too late, I wonder how to help them.

"Can't you just play along on the piano, like Carrie does?" Stephanie asks. She's the unofficial third in command.

"I'm sorry. I can't play the piano. We need to find another way to—" I hear steps approach from behind.

"If you want, I can accompany you on the piano, one-handed, of course," Gail says coolly. "Perhaps it's easier that way?"

"That'd be great, Gail," Stephanie says, then stops herself. "If Romi agrees."

"I do," I say, and smile broadly toward Gail. "Thanks."

Gail relaxes marginally, and I realize she may have been worried that I'd think she's taking over. She clearly has a lot to learn about me. I have a very tiny ego. Living on the streets and in shelters can knock such things out of you pretty fast.

As Gail plays the melody first and then the chords, it doesn't take the kids long to nail the verses. When we move into the chorus, I see the light truly go on in the eyes of all the girls, no matter the age. They love the song, and so do I. I hum along, careful not to make my voice part of the equation. I know I probably look a fool trying to be a choir director, but I don't care. I stomp my foot and use my hands, and the girls' eyes are locked on me as we use music to develop unity.

After an hour and fifteen minutes, it's time for the next part, which Carrie has told me is equally important. Food. Some of the kids live in foster families, but at least half of the eighteen girls and two boys live in families where food can be scarce and not always nutritious enough. The Belmont Foundation provides catering via contributions from local restaurants. Today we're sponsored by the Sea Stone Café, Mike's place, judging from the prepared boxes. We always have at least five spare boxes, which means Gail can have one.

We move to the area boasting an oval table and chairs. As Gail sits down, I find myself outmaneuvered by a few of the youngest girls, who snag the seats next to her. Gail looks faintly shell-shocked at the unexpected attention, but I've begun to know these kids and merely smile reassuringly.

"What happened to your arm, ma'am?" Keisha, one of the youngest girls, asks as she rips into her food box.

"Hush. That's rude, Keisha," an older girl says and frowns.

"It's all right." Gail looks at Keisha. "First of all, please call me Gail. As for my arm, I was in a car accident a while back."

"Does it hurt?" Keisha looks up at Gail with concern, her eyes nearly black.

"It does, a bit," Gail says in a matter-of-fact tone.

"Can I help you open your box? It has a sticky thing that's really hard to peel off." Keisha points at the tape at the top of the white box.

Gail blinks a few times. "Why, thank you, Keisha. It's nice of you to offer." She leans back as Keisha and the girl on Gail's other side struggle to open the box and manage not to spill the contents. "Thank you, girls." Gail raises her left hand. "Good thing I have one more, so I could play the piano some."

"Yeah. You play better with one hand than my foster sister does with two, and she's taken lessons, like, forever," Dylan, a gangly fourteen-year-old boy, says.

"That's not a fair comparison," Gail says kindly. "I've practiced the piano for more than thirty years." She winks at him. "You have a lovely tenor voice, though."

Dylan blushes a deep crimson, which ignites his multitude of freckles. "Um. Er. Thanks."

Now Gail gets swamped with questions about what she thought of everyone's individual voice. She manages to give them all feedback and tips, and tears burn behind my eyelids when I notice how she avoids being the typical lazy adult who just gives blanket statements of praise without caring. This is also the perfect moment for me to sneak out and charge my LED lantern. With a little bit of luck, I can have it in my backpack again without anyone noticing. I make a quick detour to the office area and then return to hear Stephanie ask Gail yet another question.

"And Romi's voice?" Stephanie has obvious little demons in her eyes.

I give her a stern look as I rejoin them, but she just returns it with an angelic smile. Brat.

"I didn't hear Romi sing," Gail says, looking at me over a glass of orange juice.

"Oh, she should sing something. You should, Romi." Several of the kids speak as one. "Like that song you performed at the open-mic night," Lisa, Stephanie's friend, says. "'Never Enough'?"

"Nah. That's all right," I say, starting to feel cornered.

The other boy in the choir, Aron, pipes up. "Oh, please. We want to hear too. Several of us weren't able to be at open mic."

"You can't have the heart to disappoint them," Gail says helpfully, with a broad smile. That does it.

"Fine, fine. One verse. One chorus. A cappella."

The room goes instantly quiet, and I'm more nervous than I've ever been. I don't think Gail would ever tell me I'm a mediocre singer in front of these kids, but I know she must have such immensely high standards, I'm certain she'll wonder what the fuss was about at Mike's and Vivian's when they praised my voice.

I sit in silence and close my eyes for a few moments. As I open them again, I look directly at Gail and start to sing.

CHAPTER SEVENTEEN

Gail

I don't think the expression "being floored" covers how I feel when Romi begins to sing. Nor does her voice sound like anything else I've heard from either classical or popular singers. She sang only one verse and one refrain of a song I admit I've never heard. It was clear it resonated with Romi and most of the young people around us. Tears rose in their eyes, and I found myself swallowing down some myself.

Romi's voice is quite versatile. It can clearly go from frail to laser strong in seconds, and still it sounds just…amazing. Why she's not interested in a career in music, I'll never know.

Of course, deafening applause met her singing, and it was rather entertaining to see her blush. She looked at me with trepidation, I could tell, but something in my demeanor must have reassured her, as she nodded and gave me a quick smile.

Now we've just said good-bye to the kids after tidying up and making our way back to the car. I think of the conversation we're supposed to have but don't want to push Romi.

"Can we talk at your place? I mean, if you have time?" Romi asks quietly.

I didn't see that coming. "Absolutely. As much time as you need."

She turns slightly in the seat and pushes her hands in between her thighs. It's such a familiar gesture by now, I have to smile. "You're so kind to me," Romi says. "I mean, you don't know much about me, yet you're prepared to help out. I could end up being a serial killer—you don't know that."

"But I do. I may not be the most perceptive person you'll ever know when it comes to most people around me, but it's different with you." I stumble over words in my mind as I try to express what I mean. "I'm well aware that I don't know a lot about you, but that's not the most important part, as I see it. I feel I know your heart." I've started the car and pull out into traffic. "I don't mean to sound presumptuous, but that's how it feels."

Warm, hazel eyes scan mine. "It's not presumptuous at all." Romi places a gentle, hesitant hand on my knee. My muscles tense, and I want to pull over and kiss her. *That* thought nearly makes me run the car up onto the sidewalk. I hope Romi doesn't notice my reaction.

"So, yes. Let's go back to the house. You can cook tonight. That is, if you know how to." I send her a quick glance.

"I make a mean mac and cheese."

"What?" Oh, God. That figures. "Mac and cheese it is, then." I can't remember having the iconic comfort-food dish since I was a poor student at Juilliard. Memories of craving any type of comfort food after Professor Blakely's classes appear out of nowhere. Perhaps mac and cheese is perfect, as we're going to talk about things that are sensitive to Romi.

We sit in friendly silence the rest of the way. I suppose Romi feels reassured by my words, and I still need to process what the mere touch of her hand on my gabardine-clad knee does to me. If I'm that affected by such an innocent touch, God help me if she ever decides to place her hands somewhere else.

I punch in the code to my new alarm system after we've climbed the few steps to the front door.

"I didn't see that yesterday." Romi hangs her jacket on one of the hooks inside the door without even looking and places her backpack on the floor.

"Had it installed a few days ago. Feels better to know that all the doors and windows are secure since the closest neighbor is too far away for me to feel safe. Speaking of that, I think I saw your light go on for the first time last night. Must be since most of the leaves have fallen by now."

Romi blinks. "Could be," she murmurs. "All the doors and windows?" She studies her shoes and then looks up at me.

"Yes. Especially important with the basement door and the windows down here on this floor. The security company actually found an old key to the basement door above the doorframe. Can you imagine?"

"Really?" Romi's voice is weak, and she walks ahead of me into the kitchen. "Good that they were so, um, thorough."

"Yes." I point in the direction of the downstairs bathroom. "I'm just going to grab some painkillers. I'll join you—"

"Painkillers?" Romi's head snaps up, and her voice goes from weak to strong, much like it did when she sang. "Did you overdo? I shouldn't have asked you to stay the entire session. I wasn't thinking—"

"Stop, stop. I always take pills this time of day. Don't panic." I smile and shake my head. "We can't possibly eat yet, so why don't you make us some tea or coffee?"

"Sure thing." Romi nods and begins pulling things from the cabinets.

After making myself take only one painkiller, instead of the usual two, I hope this will be enough. I don't want to become all woozy, which I do sometimes after taking two, while talking to Romi.

I regard my reflection in the mirror above the sink for a moment. I look different. My hair is the same, kept back from my face with a headband. But that's where it stops. My blue eyes are sparkling, my complexion doesn't have its usual "always indoors" pallor, and my lips...look fuller? That can't be right.

I huff at myself and walk back to the kitchen, where I'm met by the mouthwatering scent of freshly brewed coffee being made. Romi has set a tray with mugs, still the horrendous ones in bright colors, and some biscuits on a plate.

"I figured we could sit more comfortably in the living room, if that's all right?" She turns to look at me and stops in midmotion. "You okay?"

"I'm fine." My arm hurts like hell, but I feel finer than I have since the accident. "Living room, it is. To be truthful, I've had enough of hard chairs for today." I smile to show I'm mostly kidding.

Again, I sit down next to her on the couch. I want to be close, so I don't miss a thing of what she's about to tell me. Perhaps I'm pushing it after all, and I know a lot of people who would do a double take if they saw me hang on Romi's every word. Before the accident, I didn't really pay attention to anything but my violin, possibly the piano, and Neill.

Romi sips her coffee after blowing at the hot beverage for a few moments. Then she places it on the rustic coffee table, using one of the coasters that belonged to the previous owner, and pulls both legs up and hugs her knees to her chest. A defensive position. Self-preserving.

"I ran away when I was sixteen. To New York. Manhattan, mainly. I knew I could sing. I'd been sneaking off to Providence on occasion before then, busking. I hated my life here, so, in my mind, I figured I'd make it in the Big Apple. Someone would hear me sing, realize my potential, and I would make a life for myself."

A part of me thinks this is not a very unusual life story. Many young people go to New York and Los Angeles hoping to make it big. Still, at sixteen? I say nothing but keep my eyes locked on Romi's. I even move closer and place a hand on her knee.

Romi draws a trembling breath. "You know what's coming, right? I sang my heart out on the streets, with or without accompaniment from other musicians, but nobody gave a shit. People tossed coins and dollar bills into my box, but no Broadway producer ever passed me by and looked at me *that* way." Romi gives an unhappy laugh. "I suppose I'm dense—or just stubborn. I kept doing that for two years, still hoping every day that *this is it*. With every glance I got from someone who looked well off that lasted more than two seconds, I was certain they'd approach me after the song was over. It never happened."

Tears fill Romi's eyes, but when I raise my hand to her cheek, she shakes her head emphatically. "No. Don't." She draws a few more breaths before she continues. "Four more years and I gave up on the dream. Four years, during which I realized it paid better to sing on the subway trains than on the streets. It was actually safer too, to a degree. I even got a bit of a following among the six a.m. commuters on their way to work." Romi snorts unhappily. "Well. You can say my fifteen minutes of fame were pretty humbling."

"Where did you live?" I ask when she doesn't volunteer any more.

"If I was there on time, in shelters. Sometimes they were full, and then I'd join a crowd I knew under some overpass or bridge."

"And your days, when you weren't singing?" My voice is husky, I can hear it, and I'm dangerously close to crying as well.

"Libraries. Always libraries. Or museums. They're free." Romi wipes at her cheeks.

"How long were you homeless?" I ask and immediately realize that I've stepped into something even more painful for her. I hate myself for being careless. "You don't have to—"

"It's all right. In a sense, I still am. I mean, I don't have a place of my own yet." Romi's cheeks turn red. "And even if I earn a real part-time salary now, I can't see that changing."

"But you told me you live on some property close to where your relatives live?" I'm confused now, and more than a little concerned.

"I wasn't lying. Much." Romi tips her head back for a moment before she meets my eyes again. "I do live in a house close to my old home. I do. But my relatives are gone." The last part comes out as a whisper. "I know none of this makes sense, and Manon's going to realize this when she needs my paperwork and I can't provide it. My wallet was stolen in New York, and I lost my ID, and somehow it was found at a burglary, but the cops didn't believe that, and I ran...I ran and...I don't know what to do now!"

I can't take her anguish anymore. I tug at her with my left arm and pull her sideways into my shoulder, holding her closer. "I don't get much of what you just said, but we're going to figure it out, Romi." I kiss the top of her head, inhaling the scent of cheap soap and of what is solely her. "And you're going to be fine. I promise." I know I'm probably promising something I can't be sure about, but I'll be damned if I'm going to allow Romi to disappear. Nothing could hurt me more right now.

Chapter Eighteen

Romi

That moment. Oh, God. That moment as Gail pulls me close, tucks me into her shoulder, and holds me so tight, I can hardly breathe. I hide my face against her collar, inhale the warm, sweet scent of her…and for the first time in my life, I feel safe.

Telling her as much as I just did about my past scares me to death. Gail didn't throw me out. Or at least not yet, and that's a miracle in itself. I sob and tremble and then…her lips against my hair. I lose my breath again. Shifting, I need to feel even closer.

"I have you," Gail murmurs and runs her hand up and down my arm.

Breathing hard, tossed between anxiety and desire to be near her, I press my face into…her neck. Damn. Her skin is so soft and warm, and she smells so good. I hide against her, take shelter in her arms and pray this will last and last…

"Romi?" Gail whispers, and I realize she's trembling as well. "Oh." Her good arm pulls me impossibly closer, and for the first time, I can tell she's strong. She holds me like she's not about to let me go any time soon, and I hope I'm right.

After a few blissful moments, I turn my head, and my lips inadvertently brush against the soft curve of her jawline. I go rigid, because I'm sure I've screwed up.

"Oh, God." Fine tremors go through Gail's body as she breathes out the words. She moves her hand up from my shoulder and laces her fingers into my hair. Pulling gently, she tips my head back and looks down at me with large eyes that have gone from piercing blue to the darkness of a deep lagoon. "You must know you're tempting me."

I'm? I'm tempting *her*? I can't speak. I've grown tongue-tied around her before, but this is beyond those other times. I just stare at her. And then it's clear that my body has other ideas of what action to take. Somehow my brain sends signals to my left arm to mimic hers and push into her fragrant, silken hair. As if her hair is in on the plan, it curls around my fingers, and I've never touched anything so soft before. When my fingertips come across the headband, I remove it, and Gail just keeps looking at me and not objecting.

I run my fingertips through her hair, gather it up in my palm, squeeze it, and let it fall. The strands behave as if they're weightless, float for half a second, then tumble against her shoulder and my face. I repeat the motion twice and see a faint smile form on her lips.

"Like my hair?" Gail moves her fingertips against my scalp, making me shiver.

"It's beautiful," I manage to say, sounding as if I haven't used my voice in ages.

"So are you." Pressing her lips to my forehead, Gail hums quietly against my skin. When she pulls back, I edge closer, and this time I can't blame my body for acting on its own. I crane my neck and kiss her jawline, gently, but several times, as once would, *could*, never be enough.

A soft sound breaks free from Gail's lips. Tugging gently at my hair again, she kisses my lips. The caress is more of a peck, a soft brush, but it still makes my lips tingle and my arousal spike again. I touch her cheek and pull her face closer, not quite sure what I'm doing, only that I need to taste her so badly, I'm ready to burst.

Of course, I've never truly thought it possible that Gail would ever find me attractive—and how could I even begin to guess if she's into women at all—I get my first clue to both those things when she's the one closing the distance and pressing her lips to mine. I, on the other hand, being more than a little inexperienced, am aware just how much I want this woman and how much I care about her. My stomach is in knots, my heartbeat painfully strong and fast, and, which I hope isn't as readily obvious to Gail as it is to me, I'm so aroused, my panties are soaking wet.

I part my lips under Gail's, not confident, or crazy, enough to be more forward than that. As it turns out, I need not have worried. If I'm more aroused than I've ever been, Gail seems to be there right along with me. Groaning, she runs the tip of her tongue along my upper lip, tickling me mercilessly before she slips it into my mouth. I meet it with mine, as it's what I want more than anything. And we go deeper, and it lasts and lasts, until I'm shaking so much, Gail pulls back. Not entirely, but enough for me to miss her lips so much it hurts.

"Romi. It's okay. I'm not...I don't want to stop. Truly. It's just...my arm." Gail gazes at me with regret.

I'm tossed back on earth with a resounding thud. "What? Oh, no!" I'm horrified. "I didn't mean to hurt you, I—"

"Stop." Gail gives my hair a gentle tug. "You didn't hurt me. I managed that on my own." She's out of breath, and I can feel her words against my skin. "For the first time since the accident, I forgot completely about my arm. At least until I tried to raise it to pull you closer." Smiling, Gail shakes her head at herself.

"And now? Does it hurt very badly?" I look at her hand that is in its usual orthosis, but not in a sling.

"A bit. But not enough for you to move. Unless you want to." Gail tilts her head and scans my face, her eyes slowly becoming piercing again.

"I don't." I could sit here with her forever, but my, by now, trained eyes have already spotted the tension around hers, and the faint tremor in her arm. "But I think I should. You're in more pain than you let on." I can't bear to be either the cause, indirect or not, or selfish enough to stay in her arms when I know what I know.

Gail studies me. Can she tell how much I ache at the idea of leaving this closeness, this unexpected, amazing embrace? She nods slowly. "You have such a strong, protective side. I could tell that today when you worked with the kids, and perhaps I risk sounding completely conceited, but I can see it even clearer now." Gail runs her blunt nails lightly down the back of my neck as she lowers her left arm. "Can I perhaps persuade you to help me with something? No heavy lifting required." She smirks as she adds the last part.

"Anything," I say readily, meaning it.

"Of course." Gail slides back from me, which makes me shiver again, but this time from feeling cold. "I can't take any painkillers for another four hours, but my muscles are starting to spasm around my shoulder. Normally, my wrist is the biggest problem, but sometimes my elbow or shoulder acts up. Apparently today is such a day. I have an analgesic ointment that helps, but I can never reach as far back toward my shoulder blade as I need on my own. If you don't mind?" Gail's cheeks grow pink, that hue I love by now, as it shows she can feel as self-conscious as I so often do.

"No problem," I say, aiming for casual but sounding totally out of breath. "Should I fetch it for you?"

"No. It's upstairs in the bedroom. It'll be better if we put a towel on the bed so I can lie on my side." Now the pink is hinting at crimson. "That way I can rest afterward and not have to move unless I want to."

I get up and reach out to her. Is she going to refuse to take my hand? She totally would have only a while ago, but she doesn't. Pulling her up gently, I step back and let her walk ahead of me toward the stairs. As I climb them behind her, I try to pull my head out of the gutter at the sight of her swaying hips that are pretty much at eye level. Gail is going to get undressed and have me rub ointment on her naked skin. A ridiculous thought hits me. I hope the ointment smells foul, not that this will ultimately mean anything, but still. It can at least help me keep my mind on what matters.

Gail's well-being.

Gail

Oh, this has got to be the most insane idea I've ever had. Romi is standing right next to me with the damn ointment tube in her hands, and I'm unbuttoning my shirt despite trembling fingers. Two buttons open willingly, but after that I can't manage.

"Fuck," I mutter, and I can see Romi's eyebrows go up.

"Need help?" Romi bites her lower lip, and I can't tell if it's to keep from laughing or for asking in the first place.

"Let me hold that," I say and snatch the tube from her.

"Okay." Romi's hands aren't entirely steady either as she unbuttons the rest of my shirt. She hangs it meticulously on the chair by the little vanity before turning back to me.

I don't wear bras anymore as they're a bitch to put on one-handed. Instead, I've found silk camisoles that I can step into and pull the stretchy shoulder straps on one at a time. That has to go as well. Damn, I haven't thought this through. When I asked Romi to do this downstairs, all I thought was that she would just see my shoulder and my shoulder blade. Or was my subconscious desire in play and tripped me like this? And what must Romi think? I glance at her, and she's merely waiting patiently for my next move. Naturally.

Handing the tube back to her, I walk over to the left side of the bed where Romi placed a towel only moments ago. Keeping my back to her, I push my shoulder straps down and let the camisole fall to the floor. I move as fast as I can, lie down on the bed, and roll over on my left side. As it turns out, I move a little too quickly and forget to keep hold of my right arm. Yes, it's obvious I'm an idiot. Moaning without meaning to, I clasp my shoulder.

"Easy," Romi says behind me and nudges my hand away. She must've put the tube down because I feel her hands cup my shoulder lightly, simply warming it. "Just relax." Still with one hand on my skin, Romi pulls a blanket toward us and spreads it over my legs and up in front of me. "There we go." Her hand leaves me, and I want to moan again but attempt to let my muscles relax.

"I'll start with the shoulder and move down to your back after that." Romi's hands are there again as she begins to rub the ointment into my skin. "Let me know if I hurt you, okay?"

"You won't," I say. In fact, her touch is perfect, and I'd give everything I own and then some for her hands to be on me, all over me, for a completely different reason. The way she returned my kisses on the couch, oh, God, she made me want to remove *her* clothes and devour her then and there. I can safely say that the lovers I've had never had that effect on me, and for me to feel like that after a few kisses—not to mention it happening after the accident—is overwhelming. It doesn't surprise me that Romi is the type of person who doesn't see someone else's physical imperfection as a variable when it comes to desire. I may have been such a person once, I'm ashamed to admit, but I hope I'm not anymore.

Another, more important, thought makes me flinch, and of course Romi lets go instantly.

"Too hard?" she asks worriedly.

"No. It's really helping. Please, go on," I say absentmindedly. I've been so busy processing our mutual physical attraction that I haven't given a single thought to the fact that said desire interrupted Romi when she was finally confiding in me. How could I let that happen? Yes, she was just as into it as I was, but her emotions should be, no, *are* so much more important than mine. What does she think of this situation? Is she relieved, sort of saved by the bell, or disappointed? Or did she kiss me on the neck to distract me? No. No, that goes against everything I've learned about Romi so far. If she didn't want to talk anymore, she could have just left, right?

"You're tensing up, Gail," Romi says, and the tender worry in her voice reassures me. "I'm moving down to your shoulder blade now. I think your shoulder's had enough."

I'll never get enough of her touch. The thought passes through my brain with certainty before I realize it. Romi warms up more ointment in her hands and caresses me as much as she massages the pain relief into my skin. "It feels good," I say quietly. "Thank you."

"My pleasure," Romi says and then coughs. "No pun intended."

"Don't make me laugh." I smile at her save.

"I'll be boring as all hell if it keeps your pain away." Romi maintains the rhythm, and to my surprise, I really can fully relax, even if some of my more relentless body parts insist that I pull her onto the bed with me and rip her clothes off.

"That's it. Good." Romi keeps the caresses going until I'm close to drifting off to sleep. "All done." She tugs the blanket up around me. "Take a nap."

"Don't go," I whisper as sleep begin to claim me.

"I'll be downstairs preparing our dinner." Romi sounds closer, and then I feel her lips against my temple in a gentle kiss. "I promise."

And I trust her.

CHAPTER NINETEEN

Romi

When Gail comes down to have dinner, I can tell she has regrouped. She eats my mac and cheese politely, but clearly without much appetite. I try to understand what's going on in her head, why she's so distant after the intimacy we shared earlier today. Feeling subdued as well, I struggle to finish my plate, something I never would have thought possible, having been constantly hungry for so long.

I place my utensils on my empty plate and lean back. "Do you regret it?" I ask, deciding to clear the air even if it scares me. She may just answer yes to that question, and then my world will crumble. Again.

"What? What do you—oh." Gail puts her fork down too. "You mean us kissing."

"Yes."

"Yes and no." Gail looks at me with even eyes as my heart begins to flake away with every single beat.

"How do you mean?" I manage to say without allowing my voice to tremble.

"You must know that I find you so damn attractive." Gail sighs. "Being in your arms, and kissing you, was…wonderful."

That doesn't sound too bad, but she's still so serious. "Yes."

It's all I can say since I'm clueless as to what she's trying to get across.

Rubbing her temples with her thumb and index finger for a moment, Gail then runs her hand over her face. "I didn't invite you here to seduce you." Now she actually squirms on her chair.

I'm speechless. Probably gaping too. Then my words return to me, and I'm not sure if I should give in to the weird laughter that bubbles in my chest or become angry. "Seduce me? What the hell do you mean by that?" Okay, so anger it is.

Gail flinches and looks as if I slapped her. This response stirs the all-too-familiar guilt that I thought I was ridding myself of. I was just starting to feel better for not hiding in her basement without her knowing, and now her demeanor makes me revisit my guilt and self-loathing. "I know it's a weird way to put it," Gail says and plays with the napkin on the table with jerky movements. "Still, it's the truth. I had no ulterior motives."

"Stop it," I say, snarling. "Have you forgotten that I started it?"

It's Gail's turn to gape. Only for a second, but still. "I kissed you."

"I kissed you on the neck first. And touched your hair. And, damn it, I kissed you *back*." How dare she minimize how I felt and somehow claim the role of the aggressor?

Gail looks at me for several year-long seconds, and then her features soften. A faint smile appears at the corners of her mouth, and she slumps back against the chair. "Yes. You did. I do know it was entirely mutual. Of course I do."

I open my mouth to speak, but she holds up her hand.

"Wait." Gail inhales deeply. "What I was so clumsily trying to say is that we were supposed to talk about you—about something that clearly is hard for you to discuss. I really wanted to listen to you, for you to know I'm interested in what you have to say. Instead, we ended up, um…" She flushes her usual pink.

"Making out?" I suggest, finally able to relax as well.

"For lack of better words." Sending her gaze up toward the

ceiling, Gail snorts softly. "But yes. That. *And*, then you end up taking care of me instead of the other way around, with me half naked."

"Which I'll do again whenever you need it." I reach out for her hand across the kitchen table. She takes mine lingeringly. "I haven't had so many chances to be helpful to someone before. Being homeless, I was always on the receiving end of charity, of people's kindness."

"Am I to be your charity now, you mean?" Gail still smiles, but a tiny frown mars her forehead.

"Are you kidding me?" I squeeze her hand. "You're far too hot for that." I crinkle my nose at her.

"I'm hot, eh?" Gail laces her fingers with mine, and now my heart is beating twice as fast as normal.

"Scorching," I whisper huskily.

Gail raises our joined hands and kisses my knuckles. "Romi…"

"And I hear you." I hope I don't have to explain further since that will take us back to our heart-to-heart on the couch, and there's no way I can continue tonight. I've already shared more with Gail than I've done with anyone.

"Promise me you won't worry anymore about Manon." Gail studies me closely. "It'll work out."

I'm not so sure, but that's hardly surprising since the last six years have included a long row of things not working out. It's not surprising that I fear going under when this thing with Gail doesn't last. Fatalistic, I know, but…that's how I feel.

"Let me put this in the dishwasher, and then I have to go home." The word "home" leaves a bitter taste in my mouth, but I need to keep up that particular part of the charade.

"Why don't you stay? It's pitch-black now and—" Gail is still holding my hand. "You can have the guest room I arranged for Neill and Laurence. Please."

Oh, shit. No. "I can't," I say, forcing lightness into my voice. "And besides, you've spent most of today with me anyway."

"What if I said that's not enough?" The tension has returned to Gail's eyes. "I know. Odd that I should even think that, right? Considering I escaped to this house to get away from people."

"See? And now I'm overstaying my welcome." I'm shaking now. Can Gail feel how frantic I am? Doesn't she realize how much I want to stay here with her, out in the open and not like a fucking stalker in the basement?

"If you insist on going home, I suppose I can't make you stay. I wish you'd change your mind, though." Gail looks at our hands. "You're trembling. And you're cold." Paling, she snaps her eyes back up to meet mine. "You don't think I'm planning to drag some information out of you that you're not ready to volunteer? That's not it at all."

I'm a horrible person. Why am I struggling against something I want more than anything and thus hurting the woman I love— "Shit." I had no idea. Or did I? I care about Gail. I clearly more than care. I've fallen in love with her, which isn't a good thing. No way in hell is this going to end well, yet she pulls me in, inch by inch, laying claim to my heart without any effort at all.

"Romi?" Gail stares at me.

I realize that my "shit" must have crossed my lips. Damage control. "I don't think that at all. I promise." I have to get out of here.

"It's not a matter of charity either." Gail looks worried now. "But I won't force you, naturally."

That does it. I'm going to hell no matter how I try to figure this out. Hurting Gail in the process was never part of my plan. "Okay. Why not?"

Blinking, no doubt taken aback by my sudden change of mind, Gail squeezes my hand again before letting go. "All right. Good. We could watch some TV before bedtime if you'd like?"

That sounds like perfection to me. Gail and a large TV set. "I'd like that," I say as I get up and start loading the dishwasher. When Gail doesn't answer, I glance at her over my shoulder where she sits at the table, looking slightly shell-shocked.

I have no idea what's going through her head but keep working until the kitchen is restored to its usual pristine order. The chores help me center myself and find my bearings as I'm about to end up on the living-room couch with Gail again.

Gail

I don't regret asking Romi to spend the night, but I keep waking up, startled by perceived sounds. Why am I this jittery? Of course, I know part of the answer to that question. I'm still rattled for, in my opinion, taking it too far with Romi, even if she clearly doesn't regard it that way. In fact, when I attempted to apologize, she seemed offended in a way I'm still trying to figure out.

Groaning, I sit up and swing my legs over the edge of the bed. I carefully slip on my robe and head out into the hallway. The door to the guest room is slightly ajar, and I tiptoe over and peer through the crack. I can see the top third of the queen-size guest bed. Romi's dark hair contrasts sharply against the white pillowcase. She's deeply burrowed under the duvet and is holding on to another pillow with her right arm.

I stand there, listening to the even breaths that show she's asleep. Every now and then she jerks, or the arm around the pillow moves restlessly. So, yes, she sleeps, but it feels as if her rest is a bit uneasy.

I walk to the bathroom and contemplate filling the tub. A bath is my go-to remedy on nights like these, but the old pipes in the farmhouse make a lot of noise. I don't want to wake Romi up. Ha. That's half a lie. The selfish part of me wants to crawl into bed with Romi, snuggle close to her, and have some warmth restored to my body. My other half, the unselfish part of me, somehow feels that she has trouble sleeping similar to mine. What a careless bitch I'd be if I acted on my own insignificant urges.

I turn on the warm-water tap to my left and keep the faucet on a mere trickle to not make the pipes go clonk in the night. When the warm water has marginally helped me feel more human, I dry my hand and exit the bathroom. I pass the guest room, and of course I can't stop myself from peering inside again. Romi has shifted and curled up into a tight fetal position. I can tell she's shivering, and I can't merely pass her by. I walk up to the bed, careful not to startle her out of a potential nightmare, if that's what this is. The cold light of the moon relentlessly illuminates her face. Damp streaks glisten on her cheeks, her lips tremble, and I can see her eyes dart back and forth in a mad tempo under her thin, bluish eyelids. Yes, a nightmare.

I sit down on the side of the bed and place my left hand on her trembling shoulder. If I can nudge her out of her nightmare without waking her up, that would preferable.

"Shh," I say in a low voice. "Just a dream, Romi. Just a dream."

Romi keens and squirms, ending up with her head on my thigh. I cradle her as best I can, moving my hand up and down her back. She's wearing one of my flannel sleep shirts, and it's entirely too big for her. Ignoring that I'm growing increasingly cold sitting here on her bed, I keep caressing her, keep murmuring terms of endearment. Eventually she relaxes and shifts again, slipping off my leg. I feel our separation acutely, but knowing she's calm now and hopefully over what plagued her in the night makes it all right.

I pull the covers up over her, giving her back the pillow she's knocked onto the floor. She tugs it close, and just as I'm about to round the bed and go back to my room, I hear her whisper.

"Sorry, Gail. Forgive me."

For a moment I think she's awake and somehow apologizing for some perceived idea that she's disturbed me. Then I see that her eyes are closed and her breathing even. Was I in her dream before? Or merely now? The previous possibility worries me, as I would never want to be part of her nightmares. The idea of causing this woman pain, something she's clearly lived through enough as it is, makes my stomach clench.

Back in my bedroom, I crawl into my, by now, cold bed. I'll probably end up like my old aunt with a bed full of heating pads one day. Closing my eyes, I can see the worrisome image of Romi in the torment of a night terror, and I feel the sensation of her thin body under flannel against my palm. I press my good hand against my chest as a way of holding her closer, and unfathomably, I drift off to sleep.

CHAPTER TWENTY

Romi

Manon's office at the Belmont Center seems like the only calm place in a roaring sea. The elegant woman, so poised and classy, sits at her desk, reading from her laptop when I stop just on the threshold. I tentatively rap my fingers on the doorframe.

Manon looks up and smiles when she sees me. "Romi. Just the person I want to talk to."

I cringe but force a smile as I take a few steps closer. "Hello, Manon."

"Take a seat." Manon points toward the visitor's chair at the short end of her desk. Sitting down, I get a horrible déjà vu from when I sat down at the policewoman's desk after being wrongly arrested. I can't stop a shudder, which of course Manon doesn't miss. "Are you all right?" she asks, her expression turning serious.

"I'm fine, thank you." I paste on my best broad smile.

"Hmm. All right." Manon gives me a doubtful look but then pulls out a folder. "I have the evaluation slips the choir members filled out anonymously last week." She looks pleased, which is a huge relief. "I have to say you are a big hit among them. I'm so grateful that you've managed to shoulder most of Carrie's assignments."

"I'm just sorry she's not doing so well." I truly am.

"Yes. It's sad that both she and her husband are having health problems. At least she's insured via us, which covers her husband as well." Manon shakes her head. "That's part of what I want to talk to you about. As we're tasking you with increasingly more to do and longer hours, we need to look into insurance, etcetera for you as well."

I merely stare at her. No, this can't be happening. Not yet. "I'm doing okay like this," I say, trying to sound casual, but my hands are unsteady enough for me to hide them between my knees.

"Excuse me?" Manon blinks. She then leans back in her chair and crosses her legs. "You must have figured out that you're working more than thirty hours per week by now. All the administrative work around the choir and the kids alone adds up."

"Yes, but—"

"We have rules and regulations regarding this type of situation. As the head of the Belmont Foundation, I'm obligated to make sure my employees are taken care of. Clearly, as the foundation employs several thousand people, I normally don't micromanage, but you and I have a personal connection, as you were more or less cajoled into taking this job. And we both know I don't have all the information about you that I need—don't we?"

"Yes," I whisper. "I just wish you wouldn't push this point. I know I could do the same job in less time, and that way you wouldn't have to worry that I work more than thirty hours." I'm being pathetic and reasoning like an idiot, I know that, but my panic button is pressed so hard, it's stuck. I was supposed to discuss some of this with Gail, but during the two weeks since I spent the night at her house, we've both taken a step back somehow. We've talked, mostly on the phone, but our interaction has been stilted, with undercurrents I can't decipher.

She's been busy attending physio- and occupational therapy three times a week, and Manon's right. I've been working longer and longer days. Who knew that being a choir director employed by a foundation meant more than rehearsing songs a few afternoons every week? I'm expected to take part in meetings and keep records of the kids and their progress, not only vocally, but in our special social setting. And then there are the parents, guardians, and foster parents that need updates, schedules, and general information.

"What happened to you, Romi?" Manon asks, pushing her chair closer to mine. She gently pulls my hands free from where I try to hide them and holds them between hers. "And before you answer, don't forget that there isn't much I haven't heard yet. People on my staff, people who apply for grants or scholarships, and the participants in any of the classes we teach or group sessions we hold, they all have their story. Not much shocks me these days."

I'm torn between running out of the building and finally coming clean about my past. If I run, that means running from Gail, the kids, and my new friends. If I tell the truth, I could face the same outcome. All right. What do I have to lose?

"I was arrested in New York for a crime I didn't commit," I say, speaking so fast I trip over the words.

"All right." Manon pulls a legal pad closer and picks up a fancy-looking pen. "When was this?"

"Early August." I want to howl at the moon.

"And what happened after your arrest?" Manon jots down more notes.

"I...I ran," I whisper. "I panicked and ran." I can envision the worn-down precinct, hear the shouts, and see the drug-happy guy who cheered me on when I walked out the door.

"You were out on bail?" Manon asks kindly.

"What? No." How the hell do I explain this? "I was about to get cuffed to the desk..." I free my right hand and touch the side of Manon's dark-wood desk. Whereas the cop's work station had been scratched and cluttered, Manon's is polished and organized, and smells of citrus. And nowhere to cuff anyone, naturally.

"Romi? Go on," Manon says, squeezing my other hand.

"There was a fight when they brought some guys into the police station. The cop in charge of me didn't have time to cuff me to the desk—and I saw my chance. My only chance, as I considered it. They had my stolen wallet. She said they found it at the scene of a burglary at some super-rich person's house. I was never there. I'm not a criminal." Tears overflow and I can't help but sob, despite hating my outburst. "I can't prove it, but it wasn't me."

"I see." Manon sounds noncommittal and keeps taking notes. I can't decipher her expression. "And where were you staying? Your New York address, is that your latest before you came here?"

"No." I pull myself together by pinching my thigh. "Shelters." I hear my voice, so flat and yet echoing in my head, give the information required. "Under overpasses or bridges. Public restrooms."

Manon lowers the pen. "In other words, you were homeless." Compassion, but not pity, thank God, shines in her eyes. "For how long?"

"More than six years. Ever since I left East Quay." There. It's out in the open. I can't imagine what's going to happen now. Not because there aren't obvious courses of action for Manon, but because my brain just can't process it. I wipe at my wet cheeks, and Manon pushes a box of tissues toward me.

"Let me make a phone call." Manon stands and pours two glasses of mineral water. "Here you go."

I sip the carbonated water and cough when it tickles my clenched throat. I can't imagine who she's going to call. The authorities? Gail? No, why would she? She knows nothing of the complicated feelings Gail and I have tried to navigate—with varying results. Is she calling someone in New York? I careen from sheer panic to this strange, unexpected calm in mere moments. So, this is it. My past, which really isn't that far away, catches up with me, and my very short stint as a person with a future comes to an end.

"Romi? Romi." Before dialing, Manon puts down her phone again. "You're not going to faint on me, are you?" Taking the hand not clutching the glass in hers again, she squeezes it firmly. Her warm skin feels so hot against my icy fingers. "Hey. Listen to me. I know you have very little reason to trust anyone after having been on your own for so long, but here's the deal. No matter what, the Belmont Foundation won't abandon you. If you need legal representation, we'll provide it. You're valuable to us."

I can only stare at her. What is she talking about? Why won't the foundation just drop me like hot potato if they think I may be a criminal? "Surely I can't be around the kids when—"

"Romi, I've been doing this type of work for a very long time. I've met people from all walks of life, some of them with a record and some just down on their luck. Some have struggled with substance abuse, and others have been homeless or suffered abuse. When you tell me you're innocent of what you were accused of, I'm prepared to give you the benefit of the doubt. And I'm not the only one who has faith in you. Eryn, my wife, is an even better judge of character than I am. If either of us had the slightest, and I mean that literally, feeling you weren't good for the kids in the choir, we'd find another way to help you."

This doesn't make sense. The kids in the choir are *children*. "You owe more to those kids than you can ever give to me," I say, squaring my shoulders to find the strength to argue. "If any of them were my child, I'd be very concerned if the foundation didn't do their best to run a background check on the adult in charge of their well-being."

Manon smiles broadly.

"What?" I'm starting to get annoyed. What's going on here? Why do I feel I'm the only one making any sort of sense?

"You just proved my point. If you were actually guilty of anything, I don't think you'd push for a background check."

I scoff. "Unless I was trying to blow smoke up your..." I

stop myself in time, which is a good thing as I don't want to shock the posh Manon.

"Oh, plenty of people have tried to blow smoke up my ass, trust me. Rarely works." Manon waves her hand dismissively at me and picks up her phone again. "Now. Just sit there and try to relax." She browses her cell and then taps the screen. "Manon Belmont for Detective Flynn, please."

Shit. Here we go. Either I'm toast or I'll be able to breathe deeply for the first time in ages. Perhaps ever.

CHAPTER TWENTY-ONE

Gail

I see Romi walking up my driveway, but when she veers off toward her usual shortcut, I act fast and open the front door.

"Romi?"

"Oh, hi." Romi stops but seems to hesitate. "Long day. On my way, um, home."

"So I see. I thought you might join me, but perhaps you're too tired or…busy?" Now why do I have to sound so peeved? Damn, I know why. Fear of rejection.

Romi shakes her head. "I…I just had a long day, that's all. And I saw Manon." Romi's shoulders slump. "I suppose I need to process everything."

That does it. "Please come inside. I really want to hear what you talked about."

Romi remains where she is for a few moments, but then nods and walk up the stairs. "Yes, of course. You deserve to know."

That remark gives me pause. I wait until she's inside and has removed her jacket. "You don't owe me any explanations whatsoever, Romi," I say quietly. "I'm merely interested because you're important to me. Ever since you spent the night, you must know that, right?"

Romi runs a hand over her face. "I know. I didn't mean it that way. The truth is, if I can't share it with you, then who can I tell?" She steps closer and caresses my cheek. "I've been on my own so long. Not used to sharing."

"You and me both," I say and hold her hand against me. "Hungry?"

"You're always trying to feed me." Romi's smile is one of those rare ones that engages her eyes, when she lets her guard down.

"Purely for selfish reasons," I say lightly. "I hate eating alone."

"Well, I like eating, period, so I'm game. Want me to cook?"

"As much as I liked your mac and cheese," I say, hoping she won't see through the lie too easily, "I've made use of the old, but functioning, slow cooker that came with the house."

Romi's smile fades. "Yeah? Sounds amazing." Clearly her guard's back up, and I can't for the life of me figure out what I said to cause it to happen.

As we sit down to eat, Romi clears her throat, sips her water, and grips her utensils harder. Oh, yes. She's nervous.

"Manon's called a local cop she knows, a detective, to look into what charges New York has on me. Apparently, and this threw me for a loop, trust me, Manon is set on helping me no matter what. I mean, *I* know I'm not guilty of robbing some rich guy's place."

"Innocent until proven guilty." I tilt my head. "And since you weren't present during the burglary, your prints can't be there, nor any other forensic evidence."

Romi draws a trembling breath. "But my wallet was."

"Doesn't matter," I say with confidence. "Just because something belonging to you was there, that doesn't prove you were. I'm glad Manon's foundation is helping you with this—but if they weren't, I would."

Romi's eyes grow dark, and a new shininess shows she's not far from crying. "Really?"

"Yes." I shove my fork through an innocent piece of mushroom. "I've lived a very privileged existence for the main part of my life. That doesn't mean I don't realize how differently the justice system works for someone like me than it does for you, who has had to fight to stay alive—and who is without the power that comes with money and connections. I don't blame you for panicking when you realized the police were convinced you were in on the burglary."

"If I'd lucked out and gotten a decent public defender, fine," Romi says slowly. "But I know of people who got public defenders who couldn't care less what happened to them. And since I was homeless, they would've kept me locked up. Or, at least, I was sure they would."

"And while Manon's contact checks out your situation, what happens in the meantime?" I ask carefully.

"You mean, with my job?" Romi brightens. "Business as usual, pretty much. Carrie will oversee as much as she can, as she's not doing well, nor is her husband, but I'll be overseeing the rehearsals. Unless I misunderstood, Manon hopes I can take over completely—if all goes well."

"Manon's an insightful woman. She found someone special in you, and she knows it." I look at my plate, which to my surprise is empty. My appetite certainly has improved lately.

"Thank you." Romi finishes the last of her plate as well.

"As have I." I'm not sure where the words come from, but they contain the truth after all.

"You done?" Taking her plate and mine, Romi rinses them off and places them in the dishwasher. "Wait. What have you done?" She returns for the condiments and carries them to the fridge.

"Found someone special in you." I get up and take our glasses to the sink.

Romi stops, ending up with her back to the fridge. "Oh."

I smile. I can't help it, because Romi's lips form a perfect _O_, and it makes her look so damn cute. Stepping well within her personal space, I place my left hand next to her head against the refrigerator door. "Yes. Oh."

I bend my head and brush my lips against her cheek. Her breath catches, and then her hands come up and around my neck. Romi looks up at me, her amazing eyes searching mine, for what, I have no idea. The truth perhaps? Or something else, maybe something normally not found in a person's eyes.

"I found a miracle in you," Romi whispers. "It thrills me, it scares me, and, God, I think of you all the time."

A molten heat spreads from my abdomen down between my legs. Pressing the length of my body against Romi's, I feel every contour of her petite frame. Small pointy breasts rub against me, and since I'm wearing only a silk shirt, I feel as if I'm naked.

"You're not wearing...your sling?" Romi gasps as I let my lips move from her jawline to her neck.

"Observant." I nip at the smooth skin just inside her collar.

"Oh. Gail..." Arching, Romi whimpers and tips her head back farther. "Gail..."

I kiss her. She parts her lips under mine, and I explore her mouth with my tongue, eager to taste her and know every part of her. Romi's hands are in my hair, pulling me closer.

Eventually, I need oxygen. I reluctantly pull back. "Couch?"

"Sounds good," Romi says, as out of breath as I am. As we separate, which hurts, as I want nothing more than to hold her like this forever, her eyes fall to my injured hand.

"No orthosis?"

"Yes, but a new, smaller one. I'm told I'm making progress." I make a left-shoulder shrug. "I'm cautiously optimistic since my physiotherapist is pleased with me."

"Are *you* pleased?" Gently, with whisper-light fingertips, Romi caresses my right arm.

"I am, actually. I hated PT in New York. Tried several and nobody was half as good as the one I'm seeing here. Who would've guessed?"

Romi takes my hand, and we walk into the living room. "Perhaps it's more to do with your frame of mind than the expertise of the PT?"

"What do you mean?" Not sure if I'm being criticized, I sit down next to her on the couch.

"I'm not trying to psychoanalyze you, but the way I see it, you were dealing with something worse than the injury after the accident. More than losing your livelihood, you lost your music." Romi raises my hand to her lips and kisses my palm. "How were you supposed to feel motivated to put your heart and soul into your training when you were dealing with such heartache?"

I can't find the words at first. "Where were you when I needed that explained to me?" I blurt out.

"Right there, in Manhattan," Romi says, smiling authentically. "Though I doubt you would have been ready for any advice from anyone. You needed to mourn."

"I didn't mourn. I raged. Perhaps I shouldn't tell you this, but I threw a tray of medical supplies across the room once. The poor nurses feared me enough to draw straws about whose turn it was to tend to me, I'm sure."

"If that's true, I'd say that hospital employs some thin-skinned nurses. I'm sure they understood better than you realized at the time." Sliding closer, Romi pulls me closer, mimicking how we sat that night, but this time with my head on her shoulder.

"I'm starting to realize you're even smarter than I thought, if possible, as I already have such a high opinion of you." I press my lips to Romi's neck. "And this couch is starting to become my favorite place in this entire house."

"The couch is okay, but the company is stellar." Romi chuckles, which makes me feel happier than I have in a long time.

"May I be bold and ask you to spend the night again? You can have the guest room if you want, or..." Suddenly feeling uncharacteristically bashful, I don't know how to phrase my question without sounding like I'm being presumptuous. Trying to slow my breath, I wish I knew what Romi was thinking.

"Or in your room?" Romi asks, sounding cautious.

"Only if you want to. And I'm not saying we have to, you

know…I mean I don't presume…" Oh, God. I sound like a horny teenager navigating the unknown with the girl she's hot for.

"Your room sounds nice." Romi sounds relieved, but I also detect nerves beneath her words.

"Romi?" I sit up to look into her eyes. "I haven't had a lover for quite some time. Too caught up in my career, and then the accident. I'm in no position to pretend to be the most experienced one, even if I'm older." Great. That sounds even more stupid.

"Oh, trust me. You're the more experienced one." Romi sighs. "Living in shelters and under overpasses isn't a great way to find romance. I mean, I saw those who did, some even successfully so, but I was never able to let anyone in that way. That, and the fact that I'm attracted to girls, I mean, women, and I always dreamed of it being special. Does that sound totally naïve?"

I wrap my arm around Romi and kiss her lightly on the lips. "It doesn't. It sounds as if you had envisioned a relationship as being meaningful and with someone you felt something for. The fact that you allow me to hold you like this, no matter how far we let it go, or not go, makes *me* feel special."

Romi smiles carefully, and I slide my hand up into her hair. "I can safely say that I've never felt anything like I do for you, for anyone else. Do you have even an inkling of how unique you are? We're very different, but I feel more in tune with you than anyone I can think of."

Romi tilts her head and runs a fingertip along my nose and around my mouth, and traces my jawline back and forth. I tip my head back, and adding more fingers, Romi seeks out the indentation just below my neck. I shiver, and goose bumps erupt along my arms and legs. "For not having practiced a lot, you sure seem to know just how to touch me," I say, out of breath.

"Only because I want to touch you everywhere," Romi says, her tone dreamy. "You're so beautiful, but it's more than that." She gently takes my chin between her index finger and thumb, meeting my eyes. "You've been on my mind ever since I saw you that first day when you moved in. Of course, I had no way of knowing I'd feel like I do now, but I could tell you affected me in ways that were so very new to me."

"You speak my mind," I murmur and pull her in for a proper kiss. Her tongue flickers against mine, and I gratefully give her entrance to my mouth. Romi's exploration of me is not confined to just my lips and tongue. Her hand caresses me everywhere within reach, and when it finds its way under my shirt, I moan out loud. I want that hand in all the places that ache.

"Unbutton my shirt," I say.

Chapter Twenty-two

Romi

I'm not sure how we made it upstairs without falling over each other. Somehow, I think I've planted a warning in the back of my head to not jeopardize Gail's healing arm, but even that's fuzzy. It's already dark outside, and her bedroom is lit only by two dim bedside lamps. Gail stops in the middle of the floor, turning toward me. She looks so damn sexy with her unbuttoned cotton shirt and rumpled tank top underneath. Her slacks are unfastened and pushed down on her hips.

"You're overdressed," Gail says huskily.

"Mmm?" I'm too busy taking in the sight of her. Her hair is disheveled in the way I've seen in commercials for "bed hair" styling products, her blue eyes are nearly black, and the best part—she's reaching for me.

"Mind getting rid of your shirt? To put us on an even keel, so to speak?" Gail smiles and lets her shirt slip down her arms and onto the floor. I know from the other night that she's slender, but compared to me, Gail's voluptuous. Each of her breasts is a perfect handful, and I can feel the sensation of them through the tank top. The thought of holding them, caressing them without a fabric barrier, makes me want to howl. I unbutton my own shirt and let it fall like Gail just did. And like her, I'm down to a cotton tank top.

"Damn. That might have been a mistake." Gail steps closer but doesn't touch me. "You look amazing."

The hoarse undertone to her voice makes me bolder. I unzip my jeans and slide them off, along with my socks. I read once that keeping socks on is a big no-no. Better not take any chances. A tiny, threatening voice that I keep pushing back insists that this might be my only opportunity to be this close to Gail. If I don't allow myself to know her intimately in whatever capacity she'll allow me, I'll never forgive myself. I can live a long time on the memory of making love with Gail.

"A challenge?" Gail pushes down her slacks and steps out of them. Sitting on the end of the bed, she strips her socks off as well. "I think we need to tread a bit slowly, considering I'm out of practice and you are—"

"Clueless." I close the distance between us. "I might fumble, but I promise to be gentle." I wink at her, perhaps because I want to defuse potential awkwardness, but I need us to not be too dramatic about this. God knows I have enough drama in my life, and if I let it seep into this room where I'm about to be closer than I ever dreamed possible to Gail...I may end up bolting.

Gail does chuckle at my lame joke, which is such a relief. Strangely, being able to relax and not just expect to fail at any given moment makes arousal roar through me. It's so unexpected that I lose my balance and sit down next to Gail with a thud. Luckily on her good side.

"My, my. Eager, aren't we?" She raises a deliberate eyebrow at me, and that makes me forget all about being facetious, or dramatic, or anything in between. I get up, move to the side of the bed, and flip the covers down. Sliding up against the pillows, I hold out my arms to Gail, who slowly rises to her feet. As she moves onto the bed, I make sure I have her sore arm taken care of by propping it gently on a pillow.

"Tell me what to do. What you like." I kneel next to Gail, devouring her with my gaze.

"Since you ask, we better remove my tank top before…well, before." Gail pushes it half off, and I help her with the last part. And then I look…and look. Her skin glimmers in the muted light from the table lamps on the nightstands. Rosy, puckered nipples crown the breasts I touched with such awe while we were on the couch.

"You can touch me, you know," Gail says, skimming her fingertips in the valley of her breasts. "As much as you want."

I don't have to be told more than once. Pulling off my tank top, I hope she'll like what she sees. And I think she does, judging from her flushed cheeks and shiny eyes. I lie down next to her, resting my head in my hand as I need to keep looking at Gail while I touch her. Carefully, I place my hand on her stomach. As I move it in gentle circles, it trembles at my caress.

"I promise I won't break." Gail pushes her hand underneath me and around my back, pulling me closer. "Kiss me?"

Oh, yes. I find her lips again, and our deep kisses scorch away whatever residual tentativeness remains. I inhale her breath. I taste every part of her mouth and am sure it's possible to drown in another person. In her.

Gail

Romi's hand moves up to my breasts, hovers for a moment, then cups the one nearest her. My nipples are so hard, they almost hurt. Moaning, I arch up toward the touch, ignoring my sore right shoulder. I won't allow it to keep me from being close to Romi.

"You feel amazing," Romi says, her breath hot against my lips. She pulls her fingertips in slow, nearly-there circles around my nipple. Her touch makes me shiver, and I nip at her lower lip. Punishment for not touching me properly. Yes. "More?" Romi smiles against me, I can feel it.

"Much more. All of you…with all of me." I'm so damn

horny, but in my red haze, I know it's because it's her. It must be Romi. Nobody else will do. She's everything and, I suppose, my endgame.

Clearly taking pity on my poor breast, Romi tugs harder on my erect nipple. I cry out, but she reads me right—it's not about the wrong sort of pain—and keeps it up for a few more seconds. Then she lets go. When she stops kissing me, I'm about to object, but her mouth travels down my neck, licks along my collarbones, and I know where she's heading. "Yes." I groan. "Like that. Yes."

"Like this?" Running her tongue in circles around my nipple, over and over, she's obviously set on driving me mad. She blows on the wetness she's created, and it's such sweet torture, I grab her short hair in my fist. Only then do I realize I may well be hurting her scalp and ease up, but I still keep her in place.

"In your mouth...please." I manage to get the words out, and when Romi's hot mouth fully pulls my nipple inside, I cry out. Wetness gathers between my legs and drenches my panties. I want them off, but I can't risk Romi stopping what she's doing. Then she does just that but moves to the other breast after pushing her arm under my neck. Her free hand strokes from my trembling stomach to the edge of my underwear, and I raise my hips in wordless encouragement.

Romi's very perceptive. Pushing her fingers under the elastic band, she places her hand in an oddly protective gesture between my legs.

"Mmm. So wet." She hums against my nipple. "Tell me."

"Huh?" I can barely think, and my hips rise as I try to get closer to the movements of her hand.

"What would you like me to do? How do I touch you the best?" Gasping too now, Romi begins to push firmer at my labia, and I part my legs, hooking one between hers. Instantly, she presses against me, and I can tell she's just as wet.

"I want to be naked with you." I hold on to Romi, my arm

still around her back. "Can we manage that without letting go, because I don't think I could bear not to feel you."

"We can try." Romi kisses me lightly and then shoves off her own underwear. She pushes mine down far enough for me to kick my panties off. "Better?"

"Infinitely."

"So, educate me, Gail," Romi says, her hand back between my legs.

I pull the leg not entangled with hers again, up and out. "Around my clit, not directly at it. Lightly, for now."

"Mmm-hmm." Clearly a master at taking instructions, Romi touches me better than I can do myself. Her slender, agile fingers paint circles around the ridge of nerves that are already twitching and ready to explode. I tug at Romi to get closer.

"Careful," she whispers and kisses my neck. "Your arm."

"I'm fine. I want to feel you against me. I need you closer. Romi..."

Moving up a bit, Romi adds pressure between my legs. She's driving me crazy, and I need an outlet. I look up and see that if I turn my head more, I can reach one of her nipples with my mouth. I go for it, single-minded and dying to taste her.

"Ah!" It's Romi's turn to arch into my touch. I curl my tongue around her pebbled nipple, then graze it with my teeth, oh so carefully. "Gail..." Perhaps unaware, Romi presses harder against me, and her fingers slide on either side of my clit and then down...and in.

"Oh, God," I say, or try to, as I've sucked a good part of Romi's breast into my mouth. "Keep going."

Romi is rubbing herself against my thigh that is lodged between her leg, and each movement of her hips drives her fingers farther into me.

"This...good?" Romi is close to hyperventilating, and in the back of my mind, I realize I need to help her keep from fainting.

"Yes, just slow down a little bit. Just a little. Curl your

fingers up. Like that. Yes. Just like…that." I start shaking as Romi presses up inside me. "Not long now."

Romi moves her hand faster, adding to the pressure. "Like this, Gail? You like it like this?" Her voice is low, husky, and so full of arousal, I'm pushed relentlessly toward the edge. When I get there, I'll fall, I know it. It's the place where my last defenses against how I feel about Romi live.

The sensation of Romi pressing her pubic bone against me, rubbing her soft tuft of hair, coated with wetness, ignites the first tremors inside me. I hold her, lower my hand to her ass, and squeeze it to add more pressure. My heart is beating so fast, I'm sure I'll faint. I let go of her breast as I need to look at her, truly see her, when she makes me come.

"So beautiful," I whisper. Forgetting anything but her, I grow tense as the orgasm builds and builds.

Romi doesn't stop or slow down. It's as if she knows, this miracle of a woman, just what I need, what I want. "So tight," she murmurs.

"So close…Ah!" I have to close my eyes. The feelings are too intense, too near pain, as the orgasm tears through me. My nipples are on fire, my abdomen convulses over and over, in a regular, all-consuming rhythm, and my clit sends waves of pleasure like ripples on water through me. My toes curl, my thighs lock around her hand, and I can finally open my eyes and let her in—let her see. "God…Romi." My mouth is so dry, it's hard to form the words.

"You're amazing. So damn sexy," Romi says, her hips still undulating against me.

"And you…" I pull at her. "Your turn. Straddle me."

Romi pushes up and moves on trembling legs as she places one knee on either side of my hips.

Chapter Twenty-three

Romi

I'm shaking so hard, I have to rest on both hands and knees as I straddle Gail's sweat-soaked body. The skin of her entire upper body is flushed, tears are blending with beads of sweat at her temples, and she's never looked more beautiful.

"Now you have to tell me how to make love to you," Gail whispers while she runs her hands up and down my sides in a strange, tickling caress that makes my breathing catch.

"Just don't stop touching me." It's true. As long as her hands are on me, I'm probably going to come embarrassingly quickly.

"No, no. That won't do. I want to know." Gail smiles lazily, she too still out of breath. "For all I know you may want it rough, or you could like it very light. Fast or slow. Direct touch, fingers…or tongue." She looks at me through her eyelashes, and her gaze is so sexy, I hum.

"Gail, you're killing me." I bend my arms and lick between her breasts.

"Look who's talking." Gail shakes her head as if to clear it. Reaching up, she palms my breasts, alternating between them, and I close my eyes.

"Look at me, Romi. Please." Soft and persuasive, Gail's voice coaxes me to do as she asks. I'm not feeling awkward, that's not it. I'm just not used to feeling vulnerable in this way. It had never dawned on me that making love leaves you this open emotionally. Not sure if I've been naïve or jaded, but I used to view sex as physical, and this is that, of course it is, but it's so much more. It's with Gail, whom I adore, whom I love with all my heart…Gail, who still doesn't know the scope of my shortcomings. My betrayal.

She slips her hand down between us and combs her fingers through the small tuft of hair between my legs. I ban the negative thoughts, send them back into the secret caverns of my mind, which isn't difficult. Gail's hand is creating magic, and I arch my hips forward, needing her touch more than I can express.

"So, tell me, Romi." Gail runs a finger along my drenched folds but doesn't enter. I spread my legs more fully by moving my knees and bend again to kiss her.

"More," I manage to say when I release her lips. "My clit. Touch it?"

"How?" Gail tilts her head and looks down between us. "Like this?" She parts my labia gently, and the intimacy in the way she slides through my wetness, so slow, so deliberate…it makes me tremble.

"God, you're hot." Groaning, Gail circles my clit, but that's not enough. I seem to be past that stage.

"More," I say again, knowing full well that I give lousy directions. "More fingers on my clit." There. Better.

"By all means." Gail turns her hand and accommodates me with several fingers pressed together. She rubs faster and returns her gaze to meet my eyes. "You're driving me crazy."

I'm driving *her* crazy. That's insane. She's the one touching me and guiding me to something I've always found so hard, so barely within reach. Now my thighs burn and my nipple aches… and Gail's the only one who can soothe this agony. Her eyes, blue-black and narrow, pull me in. I take the cue literally and kiss her again. Our tongues dance to the same rhythm that she creates between my legs. I need to touch her even more, and shoving my right arm under her neck again, I lift one of her breasts, tugging gently at the hard nipple.

Gail breaks the kiss by pushing her head back into the pillow and crying out. It takes me half a second to make sure it's not from pain. Reassured, I lower my head and suck her other nipple into my mouth.

"Romi!" Gail's hips jerk.

A deep yearning for more rises like a geyser in me, strong and unbending. "Gail...go inside. I need you."

"Yes." Gail positions her fingertips at my opening and slowly enters me.

I move up a few inches, wanting her to fill me, take me, and reach as far in as possible. I've never contemplated this idea before, how the physical connection literally makes two people one. "Fill me more," I say, groaning as she does. I can't tell if she's added one or two fingers, but now it burns just right, and I know I'm going to come in seconds. When I shift to be able to look at Gail again, I can tell she's ready again. Ready for me to love her, to show her how much she means to me. I shove my hand down past her arm, slide two fingers along her clit, and enter her.

"Yes, yes, yes..." Gail calls out, squeezing my fingers.

That's all it takes. Just as she starts to move her hand back and forth, thrusting into me, I convulse, once, twice, three times...and then I forget to count. I vaguely hear her call out my name while I try to remember to breathe. My clit throbs against the palm of Gail's hand that is still moving, though slower now. My entire stomach is tight, tight, and some sort of aftershocks are traveling down my thighs and up my spine.

Looking down at Gail, finally, I see new tears and new sweat beading on her face. She came again. Excellent.

Slowly, mindful of Gail's injured arm, I slide to her left and place a pillow half on her shoulder. I gently lie down, and she pulls me closer. Soon I'm going to pull a bedsheet on top of us, but for now, I need to cool off.

"Damn," I whisper. "That was intense."

Gail chuckles under her breath. "That's putting it mildly. I say it's debatable who's trying to kill whom."

"Point taken." I do feel a bit smug at having helped bring Gail to orgasm twice. Considering that I have only the information in books and magazines to go by, I mean.

Gail shifts a bit and then presses her lips to my damp temple. "You make me so very happy, Romi." She caresses my arm.

Tiny flutters of guilt erupt, and I push at them again, but this time they won't return to the place in my mind where I can choose to ignore them. I've made love with Gail without telling her about what I've done, how I've spied on her. Yet another deception to stack on top of everything else. I get up onto my elbow, find the covers, and pull them up to our hips. Hiding my face against her neck, I know I need to reciprocate.

"I've never been happier than I am right now." It's true, but even I can hear the sadness in my voice.

"No regrets?" Gail asks, and I can feel her holding her breath.

"About tonight? No. Never." Another truth, and this time I manage to sound happier.

"Good." Gail nuzzles my hair. "Think you can pull the covers up over me? I don't want to let go of you to do it myself."

I can't speak since tears clog my throat. Pulling the covers up, I cover her first and then myself. As I snuggle into her neck again, I vow not to sleep a wink all night.

I simply can't afford to waste a minute of the time I have with Gail.

CHAPTER TWENTY-FOUR

Gail

The entire morning has been strange, and watching Romi have merely coffee and nothing to eat for breakfast unsettles me. She insisted last night she had no regrets. The fact that we turned to each other twice during the night, making slower, more romantic love again, and a rushed, harder version a few hours later, should be proof of that.

Yet here she sits, staring into her mug as if it holds answers to some cosmic mystery. I want to ask her again if she is okay, but nagging has never been my style, and I won't start now. If Romi wants to share something with me, I should give her space and let her do so in her own time.

What if there won't be such a time? I'm no stranger to my brain asking me evil, undermining questions, but this time, it's not a far-fetched concern. If I don't urge Romi to talk to me now, what if I miss my chance? Procrastinating, I rise, pick up the coffeepot, and pour more for myself. "More coffee?" I ask and groan inwardly at how clipped my words sound.

"What? Oh. No, thank you." Romi shakes her head and begins tracing the rim of her mug, one of the brightly colored ones that came with the house.

I sit down again after replacing the pot into the brewer. "I need to replace those mugs. They can put anyone off coffee." I try to joke, but my attempt sounds even worse in my ears.

"Yes. Good idea. They're pretty bad." Romi smiles wanly.

That does it. This is not how I pictured our first morning after. I've been through some awkward ones, especially when I was younger, but this is beyond that. I'm actually getting dizzy from being torn between elation and apprehension. "Romi? What's wrong? And don't say you're fine. I can tell you're not." My heart is speeding up, and I get goose bumps for all the wrong reasons at the desolate expression in her eyes.

"All right," Romi says slowly. "I won't."

I blink. "Won't what?"

"Say I'm fine." Romi rubs a palm along her face. "Guess it's time."

I'm utterly confused, but I only nod, bracing for impact when she clearly has to do the same.

"Remember I told you I grew up with a distant relative when I lived in East Quay?" Romi hides her hands, and I surmise she presses them in between her thighs. It's one of her tells.

I nod again. "Yes."

"I haven't told you that it was in this house. Your house." The last words come out as a whisper, and she's beginning to shake.

I try to wrap my mind around her words. This house? I think back to what my Realtor told me about the seller. The estate of an older woman who passed away—was it a year or so ago? I can't quite remember.

"My aunt, Clara, lived here with her husband until he died. When I was orphaned, she took me in, out of obligation rather than a desire to bring up a small child." Eyes and voice equally hollow, Romi keeps her eyes locked with mine. "I won't bore you with tons of details, but it wasn't an optimal upbringing, and I never felt loved or wanted."

The immediate anger that soars within me toward this aunt makes me grip the gaudy mug harder and regard it with even stronger dismay. This must've belonged to that Clara person. "Why keep this from me?" I can't help but think I'm missing something even more important.

"I couldn't. I wanted to, but...and then time passed, and it became impossible." Pushing her shoulders back, Romi straightens. It looks more like she's gathering courage than being defensive.

"Why could it possibly matter that you once lived here?" Frowning, I rap my nails against the offensive mug.

"Please, Gail." Romi rubs her left temple and then returns her hand back under the table. "I suppose I should just show you." She stands up so fast, the chair is in danger of tipping over.

"Show me? What? Where?" I get up as well. My nerves are fraying as we speak, but it's nothing like the panic I see growing on Romi's face. What could she possibly have done that makes her this afraid of my reaction? Or...me, personally? No. That doesn't make sense. This is the woman I loved with my entire being last night. "Wait," I say, feeling my own version of panic stir. "Before you show me anything, I want to say something."

Stopping as she's about to turn toward the hallway, Romi looks at me cautiously. "Okay?"

This is not how I planned it, or dared to dream it, but it's important. I can feel it. "Listen. Last night...it was amazing, but that's not the reason I want to tell you this," I say, knowing I'm stalling. My injured arm twitches, and I remember how it used to do that all the time after the last surgery, especially when I was stressed. "You know I care deeply for you, Romi. It can't be a secret." I step closer but stop when she flinches. "I love you. I've fallen in love with you and—"

Gasping, Romi snaps her head back as if I've slapped her. "Oh, God."

My heart hemorrhages. I swear I can feel it seep blood into my chest, and I can't do much else than stare at the stricken look on Romi's face. How can my telling her I love her possibly cause such a reaction? "Romi." Raspy, my voice hurts my throat.

"Don't, Gail. Just don't. Let me show you." Hollow doesn't do Romi's voice justice anymore. She sounds…as if she's already gone.

She leads the way down the basement stairs, and now I'm confused as well as hurt. I hold my arm against me as it throbs more than usual. No doubt my blood pressure has skyrocketed. Romi stops in the middle of the room that needs more cleaning out. She studies her feet for a moment, but then raises her head and inhales deeply.

"I was here when you moved in," she says quietly in that horrible tone of voice.

"What do you mean, here?" I have no idea.

"Here." Romi gestures around me. "I thought the house stood empty after Aunt Clara died. I didn't know someone was about to move in. That's no excuse, of course." Hiding her hands behind her back, Romi grows tenser. The tendons on her neck are like tight ropes, and she's even paler than usual.

"Are you saying you lived in my house until I moved in?" I'm trying to figure out why she's panicking about that. Sure, not entirely all right, but… My thoughts stop as she shakes her head.

"No. Here. Let me show you." Romi walks over to a shelf and maneuvers something on top of it. Bracing herself against the shelf next to it, she pulls the entire thing out and reveals a hole in the wall behind it. She disappears into it, and then a light comes on. That's when I realize the shelf hides a doorway that leads to some stairs.

"What is that?" Hesitant, I step closer.

"A bomb shelter that Aunt Clara's husband built when they were young. She kept it up until she passed away." Romi stands on the floor of the shelter, her arms now wrapped around herself as if she's trying to hold herself together.

I walk slowly down the stairs, four of them, which means the man who built it dug it halfway into the ground. The walls look deep, and an elaborate, if dated, ventilation system sits in the upper left corner. A bed, a table for two, a kitchenette, and a bathroom—all kept very neat and tidy. I round on Romi. "So you knew about this room, and you stayed here. I can't say I'm thrilled that you weren't forthcoming, but—"

"You don't understand!" Romi raises her voice, and I don't think I've ever heard her do that. "I stayed down here after you moved in too."

"What?" I can't tell if I'm whispering or if I'm yelling. The noise in my head drowns everything out.

"I had nowhere else to go. No money. Here I found shelter, literally." Shifting where she stands, Romi speaks with a catch in her voice. "And food. I—I stole food."

Another thing that doesn't make sense. "Before I moved in? How was that even possible?" I look around the basement, and my eyes fall on the now-empty shelves. Damn. "The jars with fruits and vegetables?"

"Mainly the applesauce and some pickles." Shrugging, Romi looks away.

A hollow voice echoes in my mind. *She was that hungry all the time.* "So, how long did you stay here? What about that house you talked about?" I drag my hand through my hair, and the headband falls to the floor. At first it looks like Romi's going to pick it up for me, but perhaps something in my face deters her, because she remains where she is.

"I lied in the beginning. I left your house as soon as I earned enough to buy some, um, supplies. I felt so bad about lying to you. I hated it." She sobs once, but her tears stay among her lashes, as if from sheer willpower.

"You've had weeks to tell me this." I hiss the words, but I'm not angry. Frustrated, but not truly angry.

"No, not really," Romi says quietly. "You still don't get it."

"Perhaps because you're not making any sense." I fling my good hand in the air. "You live in your childhood home because you think it's empty. Fine. I have very little problem with that."

"Now, yes. You know me now and—"

"Do I?" I snap. "Do I really? Let's say for argument's sake

that you were indeed broke and starving. You start living here, and then you realize that someone else does own this house and is moving in. I can understand that you didn't know me to start with, but when you began to, why not just tell me the truth? Am I that horrible that you think I wouldn't understand?"

"You're not horrible." Romi's tears finally fall. "You're wonderful. This is all on me. That's what I'm trying to say. I had nowhere to go, no money, and I felt so damn guilty for trespassing and stealing."

"I don't care about the damn jars." I shake my head and lean against the table.

"It's the principle. I stole. I invaded your privacy—more than you know." Wiping furiously at her wet cheeks, Romi sobs. I take a step toward her, but she holds her hand up. "No. Let me get this out in the open."

"What do you mean, you invaded my privacy more than I know?" I want to hold her against me, but I'm so taken aback by all this, I can't process it at the moment.

"See that vent?" Pointing toward the system I noticed earlier, Romi sighed. "It's somehow connected to the living room. I used to hide down here sometimes when I was a kid. Whenever someone in the living room, and especially in the corner with the large armchair, is talking, you can hear everything down here."

My mind races as I think back. I've been on the phone sitting in that chair. Even shed tears. And Romi listened in on all that? "You should have moved out instantly, *supplies* or not." I'm being unfair, somewhere inside I know that, but my privacy has indeed been violated, and I'm feeling so raw because the culprit's Romi, the woman I...love. The thought barely has time to make it through my brain before my resentment begins to cool off. I love this girl. She was lost, lonely, and penniless. For all she knew, the police were after her, and she had no one to turn to.

"I did. As fast as I could. I have never felt as guilty about anything as I do for lying to you. You deserve nothing but honesty and—"

"Romi. Wait. Let's just take a step back and look at this in a calmer way." I hold out my hand again. "Surely we can figure this out if we talk about it?"

Romi recoils, her nerves so raw, and once again, it dawns on me that she and I have such different backgrounds. We're approaching things from opposite corners, and I can't expect her to regard what's happening through my eyes. I slump back against the table again. Perhaps we can never truly bridge the gap between us? I thought so, absolutely, but maybe I'm the naïve one? I clasp my forehead where an all-too-familiar headache's starting to develop.

"I should go," Romi murmurs, tears coating every word.

"No, please, don't do that. We have to talk this out. One way or the other, we can get past it." I'm clearly not above begging. "I love you. It's still the truth."

Romi moves so fast, I have no time to react. She runs up the four steps, and then I hear her feet hammer against the stair leading up to the hallway. I hurry after her. "Romi! Wait!"

I hear the front door open, and I know she's running. When I reach the hallway, the house is filled with a piercing alarm. God damn it. She set off the alarm, perhaps deliberately, but I don't think so. She was running away from me and probably just forgot about it. I punch in the code and know I have to call the security company right away, or I'll have them, or the police, on my doorstep very soon.

The man on the other end asks the security questions, which I answer in the way that's agreed upon to let him know that I'm all right. I chuckle miserably after I hang up. All right? Well, I suppose I can't demand that a security company provide staff that heals a crumbling heart.

CHAPTER TWENTY-FIVE

Gail

I stand in the room that once belonged to a young girl. Everything is like a time capsule of sorts, and I know I must peel the layers off one by one. I tear the sheet from the bed, revealing the bedding, which looks as pristine as the day the bed was made. The desk, the bookshelf, the closet, all kept dust-free under the sheets, speak of someone who tried to make this room her own world. The rest of the house is a strange mix of generic and gaudy, but in here, a girl lived her life, created and dreamed a universe of her own.

Stepping up to the bookshelf, I run my index finger along the spines. Every now and then I find gaps. I pull out a random book, open the cover, and see that someone has written in it with blue ink.

This book belongs to Romi Shepherd. 2009.

My knees give out, and I sit on the desk. In one book after another, either the inscription says it belongs to Romi or the initials R.S. appear. My heart aches as I picture Romi where she stood in my basement earlier, so rigid, and confessed what she saw as her greatest sin. Pale, with her big, hazel eyes radiating her heartbreak, she said good-bye, even if I didn't realize it until she ran.

My cell phone rings, making me jump. I glance at the screen, praying it's Romi. It's Vivian.

"Darling," Vivian says without preamble. "I heard from Manon just now. Is Romi back with you?"

"No," I answer hollowly. "I haven't seen her since this morning. I…I have no idea where she is. I mean, I thought she was back at the house she's staying at, but there's no light on, and now it's dark…"

"Damn." Vivian sighs. "As useless as I am when it comes to physically looking for someone, I agree with Manon. This requires all hands on deck."

"Yes, but where do we begin?" My voice shakes, but I can't even care about that. "I think she might be heading back to New York."

"Hmm. I wonder." Vivian is quiet for a moment. "Her most obvious character trait's her protective side, don't you agree?"

"I'll say." I put the cell on speaker mode and place it on the desk next to me. "To a fault." I cover my eyes. "Vivian. She…I don't know what to do. I just want her to come home."

"I know. Wait. I hear Mike. We're going to drive out to your place. I'm bringing the boys. I know Manon is on the phone with the rest of the gang. Let's start at your house and work our way from there," Vivian says. "And don't panic. We'll be there soon."

Too late. I'm already panicking. "Thank you, Vivian." I disconnect the call and try Romi's cell again. As before, it goes to voice mail. I leave yet another message, begging her to call me back.

I make my way downstairs and look out the window. It's dark already, and there's no light in the direction where I can normally see it when it's dark. Jerking on my warmest jacket, I pull the hood up and get a flashlight. I'll start with the yard while the others are en route. Perhaps I can find some footprints, though I doubt it, as it's been so cold and dry lately. At least it's not raining.

Walking outside, after making sure I have my cell, I sweep

the beam of the flashlight back and forth across the ground. As I pass the car, I get flashbacks from all the times Romi helped me with my seat belt and how I felt the first time she was that close to me. This, in turn, takes me back to our first kiss, on the couch in the living room. I'm about to continue on to the night we shared together, but I can't allow myself to remember all the details of our lovemaking, or I'll crumble. Being Romi's first, hoping to be her last, is enough to skewer my heart.

I circle the house twice, slowly and meticulously. When I come back to the front, I see several headlights approach from East Quay. I merely stand there, shivering despite my jacket, waiting for them to join me.

Three cars pull up along my driveway and then a fourth. When I see the patrol car, I nearly fall to my knees. A strange noise escalates in my head, and I think I'm about to pass out.

"Wait! Gail, it's not what you think." Tierney rushes over to me, slipping a strong arm around my waist. "Detective Flynn's just here to help."

The buzzing in my ears begins to fade when I realize Flynn's not here to notify me of bad news. "All right," I whisper. "All right."

"Vivian and Giselle will stay inside just in case Romi turns up on her own," Mike says kindly. "The rest of us should pair up and spread out. I'll go with you, Gail, if that's okay?" She's holding on to a twin leash connected to Perry and Mason. "Stephanie and Tierney will take their dog and check in the other direction."

"Thank you." I take Mike's proffered arm. "I don't know what I'd do without you."

"One of the kids in the choir began a phone chain to see if anyone had seen Romi in town, but so far they haven't," Detective Flynn says and switches on her flashlight. "Nor have any of my patrol cars spotted anyone matching Romi's description hitchhiking along the bigger roads. They're checking the bus company as we speak."

Where can she be? I don't know how much worry I can navigate before I crack. I tell myself Romi needs me to be strong, to be the protective one. All I want is to know she's all right— no, that's a damned lie—I want so much more, but I'll settle for knowing she's safe, if that's all I can get.

After a few minutes of planning, during which I point out the direction I've seen Romi walk when passing my yard, we decide that Mike, the dogs, and Detective Flynn should search that area.

"I haven't seen the little light on in her house tonight," I say. "I've never been there. Romi tells me there's no real road leading there. She's worried I'd fall and reinjure my arm." Being so damn protective.

"Then you just hold on tight to me," Mike said. "I'll let the boys off leash in a bit."

"Wait. You said Romi lives in a house in there?" Flynn points toward where I've seen a light go on in the evenings. "But there's no house there. I mean, there used to be, but—" She shakes her head.

My stomach lurches, and I squeeze Mike's arm tighter. "Let's go." I can feel it's urgent and that I've failed Romi by not finding the path to her house or alerting Manon right away.

As we make our way along the narrow path, I fear what we'll find.

Romi

Cold. Pain. Something pokes my left side, and I moan as I try to get away from it. A new, searing pain shoots through me, and I realize I can't move. Trying to figure out where I am, and what the hell happened, I first think I'm in the old house. But if I were, I'd be in my warm sleeping bag, wouldn't I? Instead, I'm so cold, I'm beyond shivering, and as any homeless person knows, that's a bad, bad sign.

Carefully, I crane my neck to try to figure out where I am. Am I back in the cardboard box under the overpass? No, that's in New York, and here I can see stars and a pale, new moon that barely illuminates the ground around me. Wait. Ground. I reach out with my right hand, feeling around me. I'm on my left side, and everything hurts, and I can feel twigs, grass, and dry leaves. Am I in the woods? But why?

Sharp images flicker through my brain. Gail's stunned look as I showed her the secret room. How she stared at me when I told her that I'd trespassed in her house when she moved in. Involuntarily spied on her. Stolen food. Lied about so many things.

I refuse to blame Gail's shocked outbursts for my running. I left because I don't deserve Gail's love. I never did. She has the right to be with someone who's honest with her. I always knew she was out of my league in every sense of the word. Was that why I waited until after we made love? Yes, of course it was. Selfish as I am, I wanted one night to remember, to be with the woman I love more than life and to be close to her in every sense of the word. I should have known doing that would amplify my perpetual guilt for being dishonest. I spent the night with her knowing I would have to confess everything and then leave at one point.

When Gail told me that she loves me—it was like a sucker punch. If I had doubted what I'd done to her, that sealed it. And yet…another memory flickers through my mind. Gail, down in the shelter with me, desperately telling me she loves me *after* I revealed everything. And me, frantic and scared, only wanting to bolt, to escape, unable to deal with all the rampaging emotions. So I fled to the old ruin of a house. And there, I stood in the house, watching the corner where I kept my food, my sleeping bag, and the lantern, knowing I couldn't make myself stay there one more night, no matter what.

I ache at how I left Gail without sharing how I feel about her. She loves me, and the least I can do is admit the truth.

I have scattered memories of how I ran out of the crumbling house and tore through the denser part of the woods to get back to the farmhouse faster. And then…nothing. I must have fallen and lost consciousness.

I have no idea how long I've been here like this. I close my eyes when I feel, rather than hear, something buzzing against me. I can't figure out what it is at first, but it's familiar. What is that? It might be important, like it demands some action on my part. I feel down my body with my right hand, but by the time I've reached the area around my hip where the buzzing sensation originated, it has stopped. I whimper and feel myself fade again.

Gail. Can you hear me? I'm still here.

I love you.

Gail

The house, if you can call it that anymore, looms before us like something from a horror movie. The front door hangs from one hinge, and debris has collected around the triangular opening. The windows on the front are broken, and tattered curtains billow in the wind.

"Shit. Is this it? This can't be right." Mike has wrapped her arm around me, and that's the only thing holding me up. "Flynn, can you go inside?"

"I'm coming too," I say, not about to let someone Romi doesn't know be the one who finds her in there—if she's inside.

"It's probably not safe—" Flynn stops as I hold my hand up.

"Don't even try," I say, my voice every bit as harsh as it used to be, pre-Romi. "Come on." Mike sits the dogs down, ordering them to wait outside. I walk with her, and she has to push the broken door out of the way for us to enter.

"Please, Gail, be careful." Mike guides me inside.

I can't imagine anyone staying in this half-collapsed house.

Slowly, and mindful of the treacherous floors, we make our way through the dirty, cold rooms. Wallpaper smelling of mold hangs from the walls like torn flesh. The ceiling looks like it may fall on our heads at any moment. I'm far too aware of the signs of animals residing in the rooms, and I refuse to imagine Romi staying here. It simply isn't possible—that's my firm opinion until we reach the room farthest to the back. When I step over the loose threshold, I notice it's not as bad as the other rooms, even if the difference is marginal. It looks like someone has tried to clean it up.

"Oh, dear God." Flynn stops where she's walked in ahead of us, directing her flashlight to one of the corners.

I can't hold back a groan, not sure what Flynn's seen, only that it can't be good. Our flashlights converge on a rolled-up sleeping bag, a small cooler, a lantern, and a backpack, which I recognize. I haven't thought of it until now, but Romi set it down inside the front door yesterday when I invited her in.

"Romi. No. No, no, no, no…" I look wildly around the room, half expecting Romi to be hiding in a corner we haven't checked yet, but the room is empty. "She's been here. Today. That's her bag. This…she's been staying here." Hot tears fill my eyes, but I refuse to let them fall. Blinking hard, I will them back to where they came from. "This is what that fucking guilt made her do." Mike gasps and takes a firmer grip around my waist. Perhaps she thinks I'm losing it. She's not entirely wrong.

Flynn has opened the backpack. "Hmm. Here's her badge for the Belmont Foundation Center, a wallet with cash, and neatly folded clothing, mostly tees and underwear." She picks up the sleeping bag. Holding it at a distance, she turns to Mike. "The dogs. Good at tracking?"

"It's not something we've trained them to do per se, but we should try it. They've met Romi before." Mike turns around and tugs gently at me. "Come on. We'll see if the boys can pick up her scent, all right?"

I'm not ready to go. Not yet. I hate what I'm seeing, but it's still mesmerizing in a horrible way. A vision of Romi, curled up in the sleeping bag the same way she did next to me last night, tortures me.

"Gail. Please." Mike carefully drags me with her, holding onto my good arm.

"So cold in here," I murmur. "She saw no other way than to stay here when she left the basement. All because of me. To protect me. Like atonement."

"What basement?" Mike asks, still pulling at me. "Yours?"

"Yes. A secret room. A shelter." I know I sound monotonous, unfeeling, but I'm down to my emotional reserves, and if I give in to the fear spreading through my veins, I'll be hard pressed to come back from it.

"You can tell me later. There, watch out for the front door. It looks ready to—oh, good. That works."

I flinch as Detective Flynn kicks the offending, broken door down. The woman's compact form clearly holds some power.

Perry and Mason sit regally where Mike left them, despite being untethered. Mike unhooks their leashes and then holds out the bag for them to smell, even opening it and pulling out a shirt I recognize well.

"Go find Romi, boys. Find Romi." Mike encourages the dogs, and to my surprise, they cock their heads at the exact same angle and then start sniffing the ground.

"They do look for toys and treats that way when we play in the dunes. I hope it works for Romi as well," Mike says. "Go find Romi, boys. Go on! That's it, Mason. Good boy."

The dogs look entirely alike to me, but one of them starts making his way into the bushes next to the house. When I notice the other one follow and that they move in the direction of my house, I dare to hope, just a little bit. Mike takes out her phone and taps the screen.

"Eryn? Look for our flashlights. Perry and Mason might be

onto something, and they're moving toward the house from our location in a straight line. Yes. Let's hope so."

"I'm calling for backup," Flynn says where she's walking in front of us, pulling out her cell phone. "At first, I thought this was about an adult who might want to leave, which she has every right to do, but if that had been the case, she would have taken her money and possessions. Besides, I'd like to get the chance to tell her the news from New York."

I can't process what she's talking about, only cling to the statement about Flynn calling in backup. Something tells me we'll need it.

CHAPTER TWENTY-SIX

Romi

"You have your head in the clouds, girl, and the idea of you singing for a living is what your uncle would have deemed a fool's errand." Aunt Clara presses her palms against the table and leans over me. "Where you got this notion, I'll never know. I've brought you up since you were young enough to not remember anything else—"

"Not true!" I stand up so fast, the kitchen chair falls behind me. "I remember Mom!"

"Impossible." Aunt Clara scoffs and dismisses my memories of my mother like they're nothing. "Nobody remembers anything before the age of four. You have a few blurry snapshots of Elisabeth, and that's what makes you think you remember."

I want to scream at her that she's wrong. I want to take the fallen chair and break it against the wall. Of course, I don't. I'm twelve and I'm powerless. Right then and there, I vow to myself that I'll bide my time until I'm old enough, and then I'll leave this house, this woman who doesn't love me, and make a different, much better life for myself.

Aunt Clara points wordlessly at the chair. I pick it up and place it neatly at the table. "May I be excused?"

"Certainly. You better remain in your room for the duration

of the evening." Aunt Clara shakes her head and leaves the kitchen. "Something tells me you have a lot to ponder."

I walk upstairs and into the only space in this house where I can pretend I belong and sometimes believe it. I pull one of the small boxes from the bookshelf and open it as I sit down on the bed. Tugging a pillow on my lap, I hug it while I look at the photos of Mom, myself, and the house we used to live in. I have no photo of Dad, unless you count the ones of him as a toddler that Aunt Clara keeps in an album. She's his aunt, not mine, really.

I do remember the woman in the picture. It's either that or I'm simply imagining her voice, her smell, and her long, golden-brown hair. I close my eyes and hear her say my name, over and over, and her love is evident.

Gail

We stumble along the path that is little more than a line in the terrain. Around us, the trees are looming, the wind making them rustle and release the last of their leaves.

"Good boys. Keep going. Find Romi!" Mike encourages the dogs regularly. "Look. There are the others. I can see their flashlights."

I can too. My heart sinks when I see that they're moving closer. That means they haven't found Romi either. "What about your backup, Detective?" I ask, out of breath. "We need help."

"Done." The urgent tone in Flynn's voice makes me sob, and Mike's arm tightens around me. I hear Flynn talk on her radio but don't pay attention to the words.

"Don't give up, Gail," she says firmly. "The boys are onto something. I can feel it."

I'm pretty sure she's trying to keep me from growing hysterical, and I can't blame her. "I'm all right." It's a damn lie.

One of the dogs stops about twenty yards ahead of us and starts barking. A few seconds later, he's joined by his brother, and both have their noses pressed against the ground. They've found something. My fear overrides any hope and insists it's probably a dead rabbit or something, but nonetheless, I lengthen my stride and push free from Mike.

"Gail, wait!" Mike catches up with me. "At least hold on to me."

I realize I must, or I'll fall. Hooking my arm under hers, I drag her along with me, blindly relying on her to keep me on my feet.

"Hush, boys. Enough of the noise now," Mike calls out to the dogs, and they grow eerily silent. Flynn reaches the dogs first and nudges them aside. I stumble over to her just as she bends over something dark and lumpy.

I take the last two steps, and just then, the beam from Flynn's flashlight dances over what the dogs just found. I see fabric and something ghostly white.

"Romi!" The sound is torn from my throat in a cry of terror as I fear she's dead. Nobody could be that white and be alive, not even my pale girl. "Oh, God, Romi…" I fall to my knees and crawl over to the still form. I touch her cheek and yank my hand back. Cold, like a marble statue. Too late for Romi. Too late for me. For us.

"I feel a pulse," Flynn says. "Paramedics and another black-and-white are en route."

Then more light floods the path where Romi lies so still. Manon, Eryn, Tierney, and Stephanie have joined us from two directions.

"Is she breathing? Should we try moving her?" Eryn asks, dropping to her knees next to me.

"She's breathing, but it's shallow, and her pulse is quick and thready. Let me check her." Flynn runs her hands over Romi and gently pushes them in under her. She goes still and makes a face.

"Something poking her inside her jacket. I can't be sure it hasn't perforated her skin. We can't risk her bleeding out."

"She's so cold." I start to remove my jacket. "She could be going into shock." I know all about that, having experienced it myself. I spread the jacket over her, and soon another jacket, this one Tierney's, is covering Romi's legs. Eryn pulls off her baseball cap and places it gently on Romi's head.

"It's not much, but perhaps it will help some," she murmurs.

Eryn in turn kneels next to Romi and stabilizes her neck with her hands.

I'm holding Romi's free hand in mine, pressing my lips against the alabaster skin. Her other arm is hidden underneath her. "Romi, please look up. Romi." I keep repeating her name, hoping for the smallest of signs.

I hear the others talk, but I don't really listen. Only when the black dog that startled Romi at Vivian and Mike's dinner party comes closer and lies down close behind Romi do I look up. Tierney rearranges my jacket to cover both Romi and the dog.

"Shared bodily warmth," Tierney says and pats my shoulder lightly.

"Thank you," I mouth as my voice fails me. I clear my throat painfully. "Where's the ambulance?" I have no idea about response times in the countryside. What if the damn thing has to drive all the way from Providence?

"Eight minutes out, last time I heard." Flynn is also kneeling by Romi's head, her fingers feeling for a pulse frequently. "Her pulse is rapid but not weaker. She's breathing the same as before."

I worry that Romi isn't shivering. Isn't that a bad sign? I don't dare to ask anyone, in case they confirm my fears. I lean over Romi and keep saying her name, calling her, coaxing her to answer me.

"You have to look up at me, Romi," I manage to say, my voice breaking. "I know you think you have to leave, but it's not true. You need to come home with me, and we'll figure it out. Please, Romi. Open your eyes and look at me. If you give me a chance, I'll show you we can make things work. There's nothing we can't fix, no matter how it frightens you. I'm only afraid of losing you—nothing else. Please, Romi. Please." My tears fall on her face. "Look up and you'll see I'm here. We're all here."

Above me, I hear someone else sob. I'm not the only one torn between fear and frustration. All we can do is wait for the ambulance and make sure she doesn't stop breathing.

Romi

I want to see. I want to open my eyes, but I can't, no matter how I try. I'm not as cold anymore, and the voice of my mother has been replaced by others, though I can't figure out who they are—loud one moment, muted the next. I try to make out what they're saying, and that's when I hear my name again. Over and over. Not my mother. Perhaps it never was?

I wish I could reply. It seems important, and the urgency in the voice closest to my ears makes me want to reassure whoever it is. I can hear them even if the words are garbled at times.

Warm hands cover the right side of my face, the part that isn't resting painfully on something prickly and cold. They stroke me, over and over, and then warm lips kiss my temple. Now that the person is closer, I hear the voice. And I recognize it. It's her. Impossibly, she's here next to me, where it's so damn cold. I don't want her to get cold.

I struggle to form the words as I try to implore her to go to that place where the warmth is. The house that used to be cold for an entirely different reason, but is warm and welcoming now, because she lives there.

She. Gail. Yes, Gail! It's Gail's house. Aunt Clara ruled there once, but not anymore. What was once a loveless space is now very different. Gail lives there these days, though she would rather play her violin in Manhattan, and there's warmth and caring and love…Yes. There's love in that house now. Perhaps Aunt Clara found love there once, but I know it must've been before she took me in. I never experienced it.

"Gail," I say. I try to shout it so she'll hear me, but I can't. Perhaps my shouts are whispers. I don't know. "Gail." I try again.

Feet shift around me. Things are moved, and I get colder again. New hands, hands of strangers, turn me, and now I make myself heard. I scream as the pain in my side, which I had forgotten about until now, shoots through me.

"Careful with her!" It's Gail's voice again. Angry and afraid.

"We are. She's on a backboard now to secure her spine and neck. A branch is stuck in her side, I'm afraid, and as soon as it's secured in place, we're transporting her." It's a male voice, and I wonder if he's taking me to a hospital, or perhaps to jail.

"Just…just be quick." Gail's hand is on my cheek. I would recognize that hand anytime.

"Gail," I say, and now my voice is husky, but almost normal.

"Oh, God, yes, Romi! I'm here. We're all here with you. You'll be all right." Gail takes my hand, rubbing it between hers. Something else touches my other hand and—this can't be right—I could swear someone is licking it?

"Hey, move over, doggie. I need this one to get a line in," an unfamiliar female voice says.

"Charley, come." Now that's Stephanie. I'm confused. Who's Charley? Oh, right. The retriever. That explains that.

"You still with us, Romi?" the male voice asks.

I try to nod but can't move my head. After a moment of panic, I realize I'm strapped into some collar. "Yes." I pry my eyes open. After blinking a few times against the moving lights, I find Gail's face to my left. I can't make her out very well as the lights keep flicking on and off her face, but it's her. She's here.

"You came looking for me," I say and cough. It hurts enough to make me groan.

"Of course I did." She touches my face again. "We're taking you to the hospital. You'll be fine."

"Good…v-very good to…know…" My vision is growing foggy around the edges, and I have to close my eyes. "No jail?"

"No. A hospital."

"Got to re-sch-t a little…so tired…" I think I hear Gail call my name with new panic in her voice as I fade away.

CHAPTER TWENTY-SEVEN

Gail

The nurses on the ward are angels. I'm convinced of this. Instead of nominating me for the local four-star-bitch competition, they go out of their way to reassure me, assist me, and bring a bed for me to stay with Romi in her room. She's asleep now after having the laceration from the branch in her side stitched up. Several blankets are keeping her warm, and they're rehydrating her via an IV. She's also on intravenous antibiotics to prevent potential infection after having a branch break her skin. The doctors say she's expected to make a complete recovery. I damn near slid off the chair in the waiting room when I heard the words from the physician in charge of Romi's care.

"You comfortable, Ms. Owen?" The night nurse sticks her head in. "I saw you clutching your arm earlier. Can I persuade you to let me have a look at it?"

I'm about to dismiss her, but as I'm about to undress and put on one of the hospital shirts, I change my mind. That, and she's been an angel after all.

"Yes. Thank you." I begin to unbutton my shirt, but my left hand trembles so badly, I can't do it. "And please, call me Gail."

"Thank you, Gail. I'm Lorna. You've been through a terrible ordeal today. No wonder you have some adrenaline surging."

Lorna deftly unbuttons my shirt and helps me get off the rest of my clothes. "Oh, dear. We have to do something about your knees, Gail."

I blink in surprise and look down at my legs. I have felt a bit stiff since we arrived at the hospital but ignored it. Now I see how bruised and scraped the skin on my knees is. I look over at my slacks that Lorna hung over the back of a chair. They're in pretty bad shape. No wonder.

Lorna cleans my wounds and puts bandages on them. "We'll have the doctor just glance at them tomorrow, but for now, you need to sleep right next to your girlfriend. It'll do both of you a world of good."

Girlfriend. Yes. I like the sound of that.

Pushing the beds together, Lorna makes sure I have the alarm button within reach. "Just buzz us if you need help, all right?"

"Thank you. I will." I climb into the bed alongside Romi's, grateful that I have her to my left. I need to hold her hand, feel her getting warmer under her blankets, and be certain she's here. Safe.

Before I settle in, my cell phone vibrates. I grimace and check the screen. Neill. I send Romi a glance but then answer. "Hi, you," I say, still husky.

"I just got a call in the middle of the night from Vivian Harding," Neill says, sounding rattled. "Are you all right? And Romi?"

"Now we are." I sigh. "Is that Laurence in the background? He sounds frantic."

"He is! So am I. What an ordeal you've been through. We can drive over right away if you need us, darling." Neill clears his throat, and I realize he's not dramatizing, which he's been known to do on occasion. I start to weep, suddenly able to relax for the first time since this morning. "Would you? I'm staying at the hospital with Romi, but if you drive here tomorrow, you can come by and get the key and the alarm code." I sob and put down the phone to wipe my nose with a tissue. I hear Neill finishing a sentence when I pick up the phone again. "Sorry, didn't catch that?"

"We'll start toward East Quay in the morning," Neill says. "Just focus on your girl and your own health. I worry this has taken a toll on your progress."

"It hasn't. Not that way, truly. I worry more for her. She's on strong antibiotics, and…it could have ended so much worse."

"That's what Vivian said. What a lovely woman she is." Neill sounds torn between being concerned and starstruck. This makes me smile through the tears and feel partially normal for a moment.

"She is. All of them are, including the cop that was invaluable."

"Good. We'll come by the hospital early afternoon if traffic isn't too bad." Neill draws a trembling breath. "And don't scare us like that again—either of you. I know, I've only met Romi very briefly, but I understand how you feel about her, so that makes her family."

"You truly are a sweet man." I kiss the phone, something I never do. "Give my love to Laurence. See you tomorrow."

We disconnect the call, and I snuggle up as close as I can to Romi and hold her hand. She's warmer now and is asleep rather than unconscious. I close my eyes as fatigue overwhelms me. Tomorrow will be a challenge. I don't know how Romi will feel when she wakes up. Will we be back at square one, or will this ordeal have brought what truly matters to center stage?

As much as my brain insists on agonizing over it all, I drift off to sleep next to the woman I love.

Romi

Warm and toasty. I inhale through my nose, and yes, that's definitely Gail's scent. I shift, and to my relief, the thing in my side is gone. I have no clue what it was, only that it was extremely painful. Opening my eyes, I find myself looking at some IV bags to the left of me. Something holds my right hand in a firm grip, and when I turn my head and manage to ignore a quick bout of vertigo, I see Gail asleep in a hospital bed next to me.

My thoughts stop so fast, I can feel my gray matter become even more wrinkled. Is Gail sick? Or has she reinjured her arm? What the hell's going on? I search my fuzzy short-term memory, and images flood my mind way too fast.

I fell in the woods and got hurt. I have no idea how long I was lying there. Perhaps I even hallucinated—I'm pretty sure I did. Then there were voices, lots of flickering lights, and…dogs?

Another set of memories connects with my synapses. We argued, no, fought, in Gail's basement. I told her everything, and she stared at me with such confusion…and maybe contempt? I'm not sure about the last part. Perhaps that emotion was more on my part, directed toward myself.

Gail told me she loved me. Twice. What did I say? How did I reciprocate? I moan when I realize I didn't. I ran, left her to fend for herself emotionally after finally unburdening my guilt. Yet even when she was the most confused and struggled to understand, she maintained that she loves me.

"I love you too, Gail," I murmur and roll onto my right, facing her. Her blond hair is spread like silk across the hospital pillow, and the dark circles under her eyes look like bruises. I keep doing it to her, don't I?

"Mmm?" Gail says and opens her eyes. "Romi?"

"I'm awake." I try to smile, but I must fail at that as well because my lips are trembling. "Are you all right?"

"I'm fine. Just a little sore." Gail shifts toward me and our hands are still joined. "And you?" She sounds very cautious.

I don't know how I can be so certain, but I know this is my moment. Whether Gail pretends she didn't hear me before or not, I have to be strong and tell her the truth. So much depends on it, and I assume she's uncertain of my feelings after the way I acted yesterday. "Gail," I say softly. "I love you. So very much." I pull her hand up to my face and kiss the back of it and then the inside of her wrist. "Please, forgive me for yesterday."

Fat tears roll across Gail's face and are soaked up by the pillow. "You don't have to say you're sorry. We're so new together, so fresh, and have so much to learn. The thing is...do you want to invest the time? You know I love you. Is that enough for you to take the plunge and explore a future together? If not, then please—"

"Yes. It's more than enough." I cough, choking on the surge of emotions cruising my veins. "I love you. How can it be so easy to say today, when I felt entirely unworthy yesterday?"

Smiling wanly, Gail shakes her head. "God only knows. I suppose we mortals have a way of complicating things. Guilt is a very destructive emotion, and you've taken on more than your fair share. You've been through so much in your life, I find it amazing that you've managed to stay afloat as well as you do." Kissing the back of my hand, Gail sighs. "And I adore you." She stops talking, her mouth opening in apparent surprise. "I truly do. No matter what the future brings, for either of us, I don't see my feelings changing."

"Me either," I say confidently, because if there's something I know to be true, that's it.

We rest for a while, hand in hand, and when the day nurse comes in, I still refuse to let go. Eventually I have to, but I don't like it. The doctors visit and examine my stitches and Gail's knees. I find out they've actually admitted her too, mainly because her blood pressure soared and to clean her knees.

"The boys are driving up," Gail says when the room is free of health-care professionals.

"The boys? Oh. Neill and Larry. They must be worried about you." I nod.

"Us. They're worried about us."

This reassurance warms me, and I let my feelings show by smiling for real. "Okay. That's sweet of them."

There's a knock on the door, and then Detective Flynn

and Manon poke their heads inside. Flynn is dressed in civilian clothes, and both she and Manon are all smiles. "Look at the two of you," Manon says and grins broadly. "Two hundred percent improvement." She kisses my cheek and then Gail's. "We didn't want to wait any longer."

"Regarding what?" I ask, vaguely remembering Flynn as the cop Manon knew personally. She was going to check out my situation in New York. Immediately a new knot forms in my stomach.

"I've been in touch, under the radar, so to speak, with an old police-academy friend in New York, and she dug around for information, also somewhat on the down-low." Flynn looks at me kindly. "As for the B&E on the Upper East Side, they've made two arrests and recovered at least two-thirds of the stolen items. I read part of that list and have never known anyone to have sixteen Rolexes and six Breitlings. Clearly part of the one percent who should be more careful to keep their stuff in safes." Flynn snickers. "What's more important is that your name is not mentioned anywhere in the police investigation. There're not even suspicions against a Jane Doe. You have no record in New York or in Rhode Island, Romi. If I'm not misinformed, you've only been to these two states."

I can't breathe. Only when Gail yelps do I realize how firmly I'm squeezing her hand. "But I ran. I had cuffs on my wrist hidden under my jacket, and I left the police station without permission." Surely there was some punishment for such things?

"No mention of that anywhere." Flynn pats my foot where she stands by the end of the bed. "Just enjoy being free to pursue life. And get a copy of your birth certificate, apply for a new photo ID, and take your test for a driver's license."

Manon chuckles. "All in good time. Now that we've shared the good news, I want you to remain on medical leave until you're up for resuming your duties with the choir. Mike will stand in for you until you get back."

I turn to Gail, who's smiling with such genuine joy, I'm

starting to think I'm dreaming. Things are falling into place far too easily right now, and that *never* happens to me. Perhaps it's time for me to believe what everyone in East Quay who treats me like a friend says. I deserve happiness and a future, and I'm a worthwhile person. I manage to thank Manon and Flynn warmly before they leave.

"I want to go home," I say to Gail, half rolling over onto her bed.

"And by home, you mean…?" Gail tilts her head, but instead of the guarded disbelief that has been prevalent for so long, I see confidence and happiness spread over her face.

"The farmhouse. It never used to be home, until you moved in." I inhale Gail's scent, so familiar yet so enticing. I'll never grow tired of it.

"It wasn't home for me until you began coming around," Gail says. "Must be love, I think."

I laugh but regret it when my side smarts. "Ow. But I agree. It's definitely love."

"As soon as you're cleared to go home, that's what we'll do." Gail caresses my back with her good arm. "And it seems you're going to be very busy working for the foundation. I better come up with something to occupy my time as well."

"Something to do with music?" I ask carefully.

Gail presses her lips to the top of my head. "Perhaps. I'm not ruling it out."

Next to loving me, that last sentence is the biggest, most amazing part of our new life.

I kiss Gail's neck. "I love you."

"God, Romi. I love you too."

I snuggle closer, so content right now, I don't even care that we're in a hospital. We love each other, and that's all that really matters.

EPILOGUE

Clara Delaney
Journal Entry
October 3, 2013

That girl. No matter how I tried, I couldn't reach her. She clearly didn't care to respect me. If she only had done as she was told, her life would have been an easy one. The farm means hard work, that is certain, but since I couldn't turn her into a citizen that can be the same pillar in the community as my dear departed husband and myself are, I have failed. From an early age, she claimed she remembered her mother, which showed that she can easily stretch the truth into a full-blown lie. Now she has been missing for more than sixteen months. The police have no trace of her, and the private investigator I employed has come up empty.

I'm attaching an envelope with her birth certificate and the death certificates of her parents to this journal page. Perhaps someone may put them to good use at one point. I have done my part and consider myself relieved of the commitment I made when I took the child in.

C.D.

Gail

I can't take my eyes off the woman standing with her back to the audience. Dressed all in black, what else, she raises her arms, and all the young people have their eyes trained on her. Romi still has her own way of conducting, homemade gestures that work for her and the kids. No doubt my former friends and colleagues would sneer at her attempts, but I would chop them off at the ankles if they dared to. Thankfully, Romi is safe from such elitist eyes as she prepares the choir to perform at the regionals.

Lisa and Stephanie have solos, and I can tell from where I stand in the wings that they're nervous. Happy-nervous, as Romi would say. I wonder how nervous Romi is. It's been six months since she took over after Carrie.

"Here we go," Manon murmurs where she stands next to me together with Eryn. "They've worked so hard for this."

"They'll do great," Eryn says, putting her arm around Manon's shoulders.

Romi gives a sharp flick with her left wrist. The kids begin to sing, yet again a song once unknown to me. Now I'm as familiar with it as the classical pieces that lived in my fingers, arms, and heart.

"Oh, wow." Eryn tosses her braid back over her shoulder. "Choreography!"

This is new to me as well. Whenever I sat in on rehearsals, the kids giggled about some surprise, but I had no idea that they planned to add movements to the singing. All dressed in cobalt blue, they move like one.

Lisa's and Stephanie's solos get the audience going. People jump to their feet and clap to the beat, which seems to ignite the kids as well as Romi. Toward the crescendo, their voices soar, and when they're done, the applause is thunderous.

As the kids leave the stage, all I see is Romi. Tears glisten in her eyes, and she's heading straight for me. She throws her arms around me. We no longer have to stick to one-armed hugs, as my pain is at an entirely manageable level now. I kiss the top of her head where her black hair now is longer, wavy, and silken. Romi tips her head back, and I kiss her lips lightly.

"They were awesome," she says, her voice husky with emotion.

"You all were." I'll congratulate the kids individually, but right now, I just want to be with Romi, hold her, and show her how proud I am of her—and how much I love her. Her aunt gave up on her when she was still a minor, but I never will. Romi is the love of my life, and I vow to show her how I feel every day.

Romi

Of course, pizza. I promised the kids they could choose where we would go for dinner in Providence after regionals, and they picked pizza. What they didn't know was that Chicory Ariose would sponsor a minibus limousine. I learned about it only two days before the competition and knew this would blow the kids' minds.

When they saw the limousine, I think we all suffered some damage to our ears from so much squealing. Then again, we were already half-deaf from the sounds they made when it turned out they won and will go on to nationals.

Now we sit at a long table, the twenty kids from the choir, the women from Chicory Ariose, and some of the parents, which include Giselle and Tierney. Gail sits next to me, and it's as if I can't let go of her hand. I suppose, when the food arrives, I'm going to have to, or she won't be able to eat. Her arm is doing so much better, but her fingers still cause her pain.

"You've never looked more beautiful," Gail says in my ear. "And sexy."

I nearly fall off my chair, and I'm grateful that everyone is busy talking and laughing. "You're being very forward." I let go of Gail's hand and place mine on her thigh. The tablecloth, because this is clearly a fancy pizza place, covers our legs, but it also makes it possible for me to slide my hand up along her thigh. Gail is wearing slacks, so I'm not being completely naughty. Just a little.

I can imagine that Gail is grateful for the many happy voices drowning out her gasp. She glares at me, but her eyes take on that deep-water hue that only happens when she looks at me.

"Just you wait," Gail says, her tone matter-of-fact, which is also damn sexy.

"Forever, if that's what it takes." And I mean it. Ever since we found the paperwork that proved my identity once and for all, my confidence has grown exponentially. Gail's love has been the one constant I've relied on, and to know she loves me, and I love her, is really all I need.

Gail smiles. "We already have forever together, don't you agree?"

I laugh. I do. Cupping her cheek, I kiss Gail, surrounded by the kids and all our friends in the fancy pizza place. For so many years, I wished I'd one day belong somewhere, and now...

When I'm with Gail, I'm home.

About the Author

Gun Brooke, author of more than twenty novels, resides in Sweden, surrounded by a loving family and two affectionate dogs. When she isn't writing her novels for Bold Strokes Books, she works on her art and crafts whenever possible, certain that practice pays off. Gun loves creating cover art for her own books and others using digital art software.

Web site: www.gbrooke-fiction.com
Facebook: www.facebook.com/gunbach
Twitter: twitter.com/redheadgrrl1960
Tumblr: gunbrooke.tumblr.com/

Books Available From Bold Strokes Books

Beautiful Dreamer by Melissa Brayden. With love on the line, can Devyn Winters find it in her heart to stay in the small town of Dreamer's Bay, the one place she swore she'd never remain? (978-1-63555-305-5)

Create a Life to Love by Erin Zak. When sixteen-year-old Beth shows up at her birth mother's door, three lives will change forever. (978-1-63555-425-0)

Deadeye by Meredith Doench. Stranded while hunting the serial predator Deadeye, Special Agent Luce Hansen fights for survival while her lover, forensic pathologist Harper Bennett, hunts for clues to Hansen's disappearance along the killer's trail. (978-1-63555-253-9)

Endangered by Michelle Larkin. Shapeshifters Officer Aspen Wolfe and Dr. Tora Madigan fight their growing attraction as they work together to destroy a secret government agency that exterminates their kind. (978-1-63555-377-2)

Incognito by VK Powell. The only thing Evan Spears is focused on is capturing a fleeing murder suspect until wild card Frankie Strong is added to her team and causes chaos on and off the job. (978-1-63555-389-5)

Insult to Injury by Gun Brooke. After losing everything, Gail Owen withdraws to her old farmhouse and finds a destitute young woman, Romi Shepherd, living in a secret room. (978-1-63555-323-9)

Just One Moment by Dena Blake. If you were given the chance to have the love of your life back, could you ignore everything that went wrong and start over again? (978-1-63555-387-1)

Scene of the Crime by MJ Williamz. Cullen Mathew finds herself caught between the woman she thinks she loves but can no longer trust and a beautiful detective she can't stop thinking about who will stop at nothing to find the truth. (978-1-63555-405-2)

Fear of Falling by Georgia Beers. Singer Sophie James is ready to shake up her career, but her new manager, the gorgeous Dana Landon, has other ideas. (978-1-63555-443-4)

Daughter of No One by Sam Ledel. When their worlds are threatened, a princess and a village outcast must overcome their differences and embrace a budding attraction if they want to survive. (978-1-63555-427-4)

Playing with Fire by Lesley Davis. When Takira Lathan and Dante Groves meet at Takira's restaurant, love may find its way onto the menu. (978-1-63555-433-5)

Practice Makes Perfect by Carsen Taite. Meet law school friends Campbell, Abby, and Grace, law partners at Austin's premier boutique legal firm for young, hip entrepreneurs. Legal Affairs: one law firm, three best friends, three chances to fall in love. (978-1-63555-357-4)

The Last Seduction by Ronica Black. When you allow true love to elude you once and you desperately regret it, are you brave enough to grab it when it comes around again? (978-1-63555-211-9)

Wavering Convictions by Erin Dutton. After a traumatic event, Maggie has vowed to regain her strength and independence. So how can Ally be both the woman who makes her feel safe and a constant reminder of the person who took her security away? (978-1-63555-403-8)

A Bird of Sorrow by Shea Godfrey. As Darrius and her lover, Princess Jessa, gather their strength for the coming war, a mysterious spell will reveal the truth of an ancient love. (978-1-63555-009-2)

All the Worlds Between Us by Morgan Lee Miller. High school senior Quinn Hughes discovers that a broken friendship is actually a door propped open for an unexpected romance. (978-1-63555-457-1)

Falling by Kris Bryant. Falling in love isn't part of the plan, but will Shaylie Beck put her heart first and stick around, or tell the damaging truth? (978-1-63555-373-4)

An Intimate Deception by CJ Birch. Flynn County Sheriff Elle Ashley has spent her adult life atoning for her wild youth, but when she finds her ex, Jessie, murdered two weeks before the small town's biggest social event, she comes face-to-face with her past and all her well-kept secrets. (978-1-63555-417-5)